D0357485

RAVE REVIEWS F

"Mary Ann Mitchell wr
which fascination, Eros and dread play out elaborate masques."

—Michael Marano, author of *Dawn Song*

"Mary Ann Mitchell is definitely somebody to watch."

—Ed Gorman, author of *The Dark Fantastic*

TAINTED BLOOD

"A uniquely twisted take on the undead."

—*Romantic Times*

SIPS OF BLOOD

"Mitchell casts a spell with her prose to make it all come out unique. A compelling read."

—*Hellnotes*

"Mitchell is able to write without the stuffiness that puffs out the majority of modern vampire novels and given the chance she can turn on the gruesome as good as anyone."

—*Masters of Terror*

"Gut-churningly good. I haven't read a vampire novel this 3-D in quite some time."

—*The Midwest Book Review*

"Rich in imagery and sympathetic characters, *Sips of Blood* is a fast-paced and intriguing tale that vampire fans are sure to enjoy."

—*Painted Rock Reviews*

MORE PRAISE FOR MARY ANN MITCHELL!

"Mary Ann Mitchell will make her readers cringe while they read the horror within her pages!"

—*Huntress Reviews*

DRAWN TO THE GRAVE

"Mitchell knows how to set a mood, and how to sustain this eerie novel."

—*Mystery Scene*

AMBROSIAL FLESH

"Mary Ann Mitchell has written a very exciting horror novel that is so scary it will force readers to sleep with the lights on."

—*The Best Reviews*

FOREVER YOUNG

"Marie Laveau," Sade said. "That is a familiar name to me, mademoiselle. Although I'm sure there is no connection between you and the woman I knew."

"Why couldn't it be the same woman, monsieur?"

"Because I knew her long ago, long before you were born."

"I am Marie Laveau, the Vodou Queen of New Orleans."

Sade laughed.

"You do look very much like her, but I'm sure the one I knew is resting in her grave."

"Because you wouldn't give her eternal life?"

Sade dropped her hand and re-evaluated her. Before she could protest he swept the tignon from her hair. The brown-black curls burst forth from the black material and the long hair settled across her shoulders. He remembered running his fingers through the softness of those curls.

"You are far from New Orleans, mademoiselle. Why did you leave?"

"I wanted to find you. . . ."

Other *Leisure* books by Mary Ann Mitchell:

AMBROSIAL FLESH
DRAWN TO THE GRAVE

The Marquis de Sade Saga:
TAINTED BLOOD
CATHEDRAL OF VAMPIRES
QUENCHED
SIPS OF BLOOD

THE VAMPIRE DE SADE

MARY ANN MITCHELL

Albany County
Public Library
Laramie, Wyoming

LEISURE BOOKS NEW YORK CITY

A LEISURE BOOK®

September 2004

Published by

Dorchester Publishing Co., Inc.
200 Madison Avenue
New York, NY 10016

If you purchased this book without a cover you should be aware that this book is stolen property. It was reported as "unsold and destroyed" to the publisher and neither the author nor the publisher has received any payment for this "stripped book."

Copyright © 2004 by Mary Ann Mitchell

All rights reserved. No part of this book may be reproduced or transmitted in any form or by any electronic or mechanical means, including photocopying, recording or by any information storage and retrieval system, without the written permission of the publisher, except where permitted by law.

ISBN 0-8439-5417-5

The name "Leisure Books" and the stylized "L" with design are trademarks of Dorchester Publishing Co., Inc.

Printed in the United States of America.

Visit us on the web at www.dorchesterpub.com.

THE VAMPIRE DE SADE

Come, pretty babe, come, pretty babe,
thy father's shame, thy mother's grief:
Born as a doubt, to all our dole,
and to thyself unhappy chief:
Come Lullaby, come lullaby,
and wrap thee warm.
Poor soul, thou think'st no creature harm,
Poor soul, thou think'st no creature harm.

—Lullaby: "Come, Pretty Babe"
William Byrd, 1543–1623

Chapter One

"Do you dream, Uncle?" The child was fair, with long hair streaming down her slight shoulders. Her eyes were wide and expectant, waiting for her uncle's answer. She had flung her bedclothes away and grabbed the soft cotton of her uncle's shirt.

"I'm free when I sleep, Liliana. Witches, wolves, and spirits don't chase me the way they do you. No longer do I dream."

"You almost sound sad about that, Uncle. Why would you miss such horrible ogres?"

"I don't. Liliana, I miss you. No one else means as much to me as you do."

"But I'm here, Uncle, sitting upon your lap. How can you miss me when I am so close to you?" The child tilted her head to the side and strands of hair fell over one eye.

Uncle Louis tried to squeeze her arm, but no matter how much pressure his hands exerted, he couldn't feel his niece's soft flesh. Liliana didn't cry out in pain. She sat quietly waiting for an answer.

"I never dream," he repeated. "I never dream because I'm dead."

"Will I someday be dead like you, Uncle?"

"Many pray for a different kind of death than mine."

"But will I die, and can I spend forever with you?"

His hand sought the smoothness of her cheek, and surprisedly found the softness beneath his fingertips. He cupped her chin. Her pale eyes looked into his with great love.

"I would share all that I have with you, Liliana. Even death."

"Will you ever regret it, Uncle?"

"There is nothing that I regret. When I've taken, it has been because I wanted possession. What I've cast off, I've cast off in boredom. Each moment is fed by its own needs, and I do not beg forgiveness for any of my desires."

"Will I grow old like you before I die?"

Sade laughed and hugged the child to his body.

"I never will be old and neither will you." He brushed her blond hair off her shoulder, revealing her slender, delicate neck. He wrapped his hand around her neck and felt her pulse against his flesh. Her neck was so tiny that he thought of the chickens he had seen his servants kill. The chickens squawked just before the servants so easily wrung their necks. His hand tightened on the child's neck but she did not make a sound, did not fight him.

As a joke Liliana stuck out her tongue, rolled her eyes, and made believe he was really choking her.

"Don't mock me, Liliana," Sade said.

She pulled free from his grip and rose up in his lap and

kissed his cheek. His skin burned where her lips had been.

"You must go back to sleep, Liliana."

"I can't sleep after those horrible nightmares. Tell me a story. A nice story where princesses meet fairies and bad men don't exist."

"I wish you were a princess, my little dumpling."

"Would you be my knight and slay all the bogeymen and dragons for me?"

"Ah, yes. Especially the ones that make my princess wake crying in the middle of the night. I'd chop off their heads and bury their bodies deep in the ground."

"And what would you do with the heads, Uncle?"

"Burn them to ash, so that they couldn't return and bother you ever again."

The little girl's fingers touched his lips, outlining the shape.

"That tickles, Liliana." He laughed and playfully attempted to bite her fingers.

"What will you do with my head, Uncle?" Her face looked as though it were made of stone. The eyes didn't blink, the nose didn't twitch, and the lips were hardened into double lines.

"Your head is attached to your shoulders. Right where it belongs."

"What did you do with my head?" Her lips barely shaped the words, but he clearly understood what she said.

"I don't know what you're talking about, child. It's late, and you are tired." He tried to lay her back on the silk sheets, but he couldn't budge her. "What are you doing, Liliana? Do you want me to call your grandmother?"

"Grandma," she sung out.

"Shhh! She doesn't like me visiting you."

"She didn't come when I cried out in fear. You did. She can't complain about that."

"Yes, she can. Please, lie down and go back to sleep and I'll promise to bring home a special gift for you."

"Will you make me whole again?"

"Stop this silliness and go to sleep."

He stood, but she knelt and grabbed onto his forearms.

"Don't leave me, Uncle. I'm afraid of the dark. Afraid of the beasts that will come to rip me apart."

"They won't come again, Liliana."

"How do you know?"

"Because you are much older when the insane vampires rip you apart."

Suddenly Sade stood in an old cemetery. He yelled out Liliana's name several times.

"*Ma petite chère!*"

"*Mon enfant!*"

Tilted crosses surrounded him. He couldn't walk without tripping over twigs and bark. The soil smelled of age and decay. He tripped and fell to the ground. A hand reached out of the soil, and he tried to take hold, but a wind rose that swirled the leaves and blocked his view. His hands were numb. They felt nothing, but his knees felt the twigs and branches biting into them. He flung his body forward in a last attempt to find Liliana.

Chapter Two

The lid of Sade's coffin gave way under his strength. He sat peering around an ancient room, recalling that he had been sleeping in a castle ruin. Empty candlesticks sat on a rotting bureau. Stripped of paint and unused for a century, the bureau looked frail, barely able to bear the weight of bronze candlesticks. Dust covered everything, including the ornate casket he had borrowed from the cemetery in back of the castle. He had emptied the casket of its contents and easily carried it up the winding staircase to the only bedroom still whole.

He had chosen to hide here from dreams that wouldn't go away. Maybe a change of location or a quieter place to rest might submerge the devils that brought his nightmares.

He had begun dreaming three months ago, and knowing that this was supposed to be impossible, he had decided to tell no one. Vampires didn't dream when they lay dead in their coffins. That was the only time they could be completely at rest. But something had changed for him.

He heard the wind whistle through the drafty hallway. The walls of the castle were pockmarked with holes, and the smell of the flowers and pollen drifted freely throughout the building. Far better than the decay he had smelled in his dream.

He leaped from the casket and walked around the bedroom. A giant canopy stretched across the bare bones of a bed, the mattress gone and the frame staunchly waiting. The posts were decoratively carved with faces that could have come from nightmares, but none as terrifying as his. The stone floor felt cold against his bare feet.

The night had arrived to rescue him from his sleep. He felt more tired than usual during the day and more anxious at night. Sleep now would only come during the day, and the night never brought rest anymore.

He tried to blot out her name, but it echoed inside his head.

"Liliana."

His niece, the daughter of his wife's sister. His niece, only his niece.

He had transformed her into a vampire while she was in her teens. A beautiful, charming girl that had never turned twenty. Her final death had come in an old cemetery where mutant vampires had torn her body apart.

But that had been years ago and in a different country. He wasn't in the United States anymore. He was back in France, back in his homeland, where the soil kept him alive.

He looked at the casket and saw mildew spreading upward along one side of the rare hardwood. He brushed it off with one hand, and the black flecks stuck to his fingers. He wiped his hand off on the curtain attached to the canopy, and as he did the curtain slipped away and settled in his hand. He raised the material to his nose to catch a scent, but the material was dank and stuffy with age.

"Liliana."

He remembered her perfume, her laugh, her voice, and the touch of her hand.

He missed her but didn't want her to return. It was better that she was gone and couldn't remind him of his selfishness.

"Liliana, I'm sorry. Now go away. Spare your uncle the pain of seeing you again."

He spun toward the doorway. Tonight he would walk the forest barefoot, prowling for blood, settling for animal blood, since he was so far away from any townspeople. And then he would climb into this borrowed coffin and perhaps even pray for freedom from the dreams.

As he entered the hallway, the whistle of the wind increased, and his cotton shirt rustled.

He had let his hair grow long, and now he pulled it back and tied it with a leather string that he kept in his shirt pocket. He needed to face the night, see the stars, bring death to one of God's creatures.

A few paintings hung on the walls, most with varying degrees of water damage, but he could still make out the features of most of the subjects. Haughty people who believed they'd never die. Noblemen glancing at Sade as if he were a peasant. Overdressed women smiling their sweet invitations.

"Liliana."

He grabbed the closest portrait and broke it across his left knee, letting the pieces fall to the stone floor.

With determination, he staggered down the stairs, brushed the cobwebs from the banisters, and forced the front door open.

Chapter Three

Marie hadn't seen Sade for months and was damn happy about it. What the hell brought him to mind? she wondered while spilling candle wax on the flesh of a very rotund male. The client panted like a dog and moaned loudly. A bit overwrought, she thought. Would she be able to bite through those double chins to find his neck? Perhaps she would go hungry.

"On my nipples. On my nipples," the client urged her.

She acquiesced, bringing the flame closer, almost touching his nipple with the fire.

Louis Sade would quickly get bored with this beast that lay under her. Louis Sade. Could she actually miss him? Scary thought, she decided.

"Yes, maîtresse. I'll do whatever you say. Please don't set me on fire."

Not a bad idea, she thought. Only, the smell and smoke would attract too much attention here in the middle of Paris. Her neighbors would be knocking on her door, and the fire department would follow. This kind of thing was much better centuries ago, when common folk were loath to interfere in the affairs of the high-born. Even though she herself hadn't been born to the nobility, she had seen to it that her firstborn daughter married into nobility.

Ugh! she thought. The Marquis de Sade. Was it worth giving up one's firstborn to a man like Sade to ensure a noble name for her grandchildren?

"Oh, maîtresse, the straps are hurting my wrists," her client cried out.

Hurting his wrists? She had purposefully bought the fur-lined straps for wimps like this fool.

Marie reached up to her client's neck and attempted to lift the folds of flesh that covered his neck and hid his blood vessels.

"Your touch, maîtresse, is heavenly. I would do anything and suffer anything for you." He pursed his lips, not for a kiss, but to concentrate on the sound of her voice.

"A slight prick on the neck to mark you as mine is all I require, little one."

The client had asked for the nickname "little one" to be used whenever she addressed him. Sometimes Marie thought feeding might be easier if she just went down near the docks, found the loneliest corner, and jumped the first human to come along. Then she could simply roll the body into the Seine and let the gendarmes scratch their heads in dismay. A bloodless corpse. What would the papers make of that? She giggled.

"Maîtresse, do not laugh at me. I yearn to be yours in every way. Brand me with your initials, lure me into your dark world, and keep me there forever."

This one was such a novice. He was far too melodramatic, not at all a natural in the sadomasochist scene. He took pleasure from the fantasy and not truly from the pain. Perhaps she should not permit him to return.

"Maîtresse, have I angered you? Have I offended you with my talk? Speak to me, maîtresse."

Marie let go of his sweaty flesh and reached under the bed, drawing a many-tongued whip from beneath it. She stood and wielded the whip over her head, lashing her client's flesh mercilessly. His cries made her ears ring. Pain no longer a fantasy, he reacted with true fear, giving her great pleasure.

"Ask me for more, my little one. Show that you are worthy to lie in my bed."

Tears crept out from under his blindfold. His body shivered, and his flesh stank.

"Beg, my little one. Beg like the baby you are." The whip crested above her head, then sank into the fatty flesh resting upon the bed.

"Speak the words I want to hear," she shrieked.

"More," he cried. "I've been bad and need more punishment. I beg you, maîtresse, cleanse me."

"I don't know what sins you have committed and don't want to hear your tedious recitation. I am no priestess granting absolution. I'm the devil meting out justice."

"Whoever you are, I ask that you make me bleed for what I've done. Make me feel the pain I've caused others."

This may turn out to be more pleasurable than I had anticipated, she thought, seeing her client's flesh percolate blood from the newly opened gashes she had made.

Now it's time to slumber,
sleep my child, don't cry.
For the time will come
for weeping, by and by.
Oh my love, oh my dear heart,
sing lulla-lullaby.

Close those heavenly eyes,
as other children do,
for soon a dark veil
will cover the sky.
Oh my love, oh my dear heart,
sing lulla-lullaby.

—Canzonetta spirituale sopra la nanna
Hor ch'ètempo di dormire
Tarquinio Merula, 1594–1665

Chapter Four

Liliana's giggles turned to hiccups. Sade reached up to lift Liliana off the carousel. She had already gone around three times and cried out for more.

"You're having too much fun, *ma chère*. Your grandmother will have my head if I bring you back a dizzy little girl."

"One more time. Please," she begged through her hiccups.

Sade laughed and hugged Liliana close. Her legs wriggled with glee, and her hands kept pointing toward the silver and blue wooden horse she had been riding.

"We must go home now, but tonight, after everyone is asleep, I'll sneak you a second dessert." He winked at her, but she wouldn't be turned away from the carousel that easily.

"I'll be asleep, Uncle. How can I eat a second dessert if I'm asleep?"

"You'll have it for the morning."

She shook her head. "No, Gigi will eat it."

"I will banish Gigi to the backyard."

"No, don't do that, she may get lost. Besides, she always sleeps with me. She would be very lonely."

"And so would you, I suppose."

A blush flushed her young cheeks. Her hiccups had disappeared.

"So you must find a way to get the dessert to me before I go to sleep."

"Now what plot could I devise to throw all the others off my trail while I pay a visit to your room?"

"Just tell them you wish to say good night to me, silly. Grandma allows you to say good night to me when she's in a good mood."

"And how can we be sure that she'll be in a good mood?"

"I'll be the best little granddaughter she has. I'll eat everything on my plate and go to bed without a fuss."

"Then we should be giving you a second dessert every night, if that would make you so easy to live with."

The skies grew dark. A wind pierced their summer clothing.

"Uncle, why is it so cold?"

Lightning and thunder came from the sky.

Liliana hid her face against Sade's shoulder.

"Don't be frightened, *ma chère*. It is merely a summer storm. It will go as quickly as it came."

"It's not just a storm. Someone is very angry at us."

"Your grandmother would never frighten her favorite grandchild."

"Not Grandma, someone I don't know. She hates us, but I don't know why."

Sade too sensed the presence of another.

"Think of tonight, *ma chère*, and the dessert. Before you know it, we will be home."

The clouds burst open with rain. It soaked their clothes and blinded their eyes.

"I can't see anything, Uncle," she cried. "Are you still here with me?"

"Of course I am. Don't you feel my arms about you?"

"I feel as though I'm floating free."

Sade tried to hug her closer, but she wasn't in his arms. He stretched his empty arms before him and cried out to the little girl. There was nothing but water pounding down upon his hands.

He heard a scream, but it was not that of a young child. Instead he heard a young woman call out his name. A young woman who had just been a child in his arms.

Chapter Five

Sade woke with a start, brushing away the leaves he had used to bury himself that morning. A sturdy old tree loomed over him. His clothes were wrinkled and dirty and his feet still bare.

"Liliana," he called.

If only he had prevented the mutants from taking her. If only he had never taken her himself.

"I did it because I loved you, Liliana. You teased me one too many times, and I could not let you get away from me. Other arms would have stolen you away. Children would have made your skin sag. Babies would have sucked those plump breasts dry. I meant to keep you beautiful, but your happiness was not wrapped up in your beauty."

A full moon appeared to stare down upon him through the upper branches of the trees. He bayed like a wolf, and he heard small animals rustle about in the woods surrounding him.

"Why do you torment me, Liliana?"

He stood. Blood stained his shirt and pants. He must have caught some animal before dawn, but he couldn't remember what it had been. He had gone deep into the forest, too far from the ruined castle to return, so he had settled against this tree and scooped handfuls of earth upon his body along with leaves as a meager means of camouflage. What did he have to hide from? Only the dreams inside his head, and leaves could not protect him from them.

He turned around slowly, trying to get his bearings before moving on. If he went north he would no doubt return to the castle. What he would find in the other three cardinal directions he did not know.

He had casually come upon the castle. Perhaps if he went in another direction he would find human blood tonight instead of the stinking animals that left bits of their fur between his teeth.

I have stooped to your level, Liliana. Remember how I berated you for drinking the blood of lowly animals? Now I too am imbibing from those disgusting, filthy beasts. But not tonight, Liliana. Tonight I will drink the blood of the prettiest virgin. . . . Ah, but they are so hard to find and such a bore when one attempts to arouse their interest. No, the woman shall be a strong mother with children aplenty and blood hot from the births and drudgery of her days. Her hips will be ample, her breasts swollen with milk, and her breath, although not sweet, will at least be human.

Sade came upon a farmhouse of substantial size. The animals were tucked away in the barn, except for the golden retriever whose tail wagged frantically at the sight of Sade.

"I hope you earn your board by corralling the animals, else you should be shot between those bright happy eyes."

The lights were out in the main house, and several windows were open, letting in the chill of the night.

"A hearty family, no doubt," he said, walking closer to one of the windows to peer in. Two sleeping children slept in trundle beds. The children could not have been more than five and six, and each had his arms wrapped around a furry toy.

Too small, he thought, as he turned toward another window. Inside, a bald male figure lay on his side, the blankets pulled up to his chin. He slept alone and used the center part of the mattress. Certainly a male who was not used to sharing, Sade thought. He was about to turn away in disappointment when he spied a photograph on the night table. Two boys from the previous room stood in front of an adolescent with long, slender limbs and an ample bosom, her only flaw the braces on her teeth.

Perhaps there is a treasure to be found within the walls of this house. He reached through the window and easily lifted the photograph from the night table. The silver frame had several scratches on its smooth surface and the glass covering the photograph was missing. Sade ripped the photograph out and let the frame drop to the ground.

The girl was wearing shorts and a peasant-style blouse. She rested her hands on the boys' heads and each boy wrapped an arm around her hips.

Sade doubted that a baby-sitter would take up space on a parent's night table.

He heard the soft murmurs made by one of the boys, and carefully returned to the window in the boys' room.

He watched the door open, and an adolescent dressed in an undershirt and light cotton shorts stepped into the room.

"Hush, Davie. Dad will be furious if you wake him." She arrived at the lowest mattress and retrieved the blanket from the foot of the bed. "You must be cold." She bundled the boy in the blanket and shivered herself. "Father and his healthy air."

Sade pulled back quickly when he saw her turn toward the window. A few seconds later the window was closed, the latch clicked shut.

He no longer heard any whisperings. He dipped below the windowsill, coming to full height only after he was sure that she could not see him.

When he reached the front porch, the retriever greeted him again with a wagging tail.

"What, no sign warning, '*Attention, chien méchant*'? I take that to mean that strangers have nothing to fear from you. Sit." The dog immediately obeyed. "Lie down." The dog stretched out its forelegs and rested his head on his paws. "You are much better behaved than my Liliana's Gigi."

Sade walked to the front door, turned the knob, and pushed. The door slowly and quietly opened. He heard the patter of feet in the hall to his right. A soft chuckle was quickly hushed. He closed the door, locking out the retriever, who had started to follow.

The main room contained old furniture. Not antiques, just old. He guessed that the father had inherited the house from his parents and had never bothered to replace the furniture. The throw rug in the hallway was threadbare, allowing the shine of the floor tiles to peek through.

"Night," he heard, and then a door was closed.

"Brrrr," the girl muttered. Her feet shuffled across the cold tiles. "Damn, we should have set a small fire in the fireplace before going to bed."

Sade waited as the voice came closer. When he could hear that she was about to round a corner, he backed up into the shadows of the hallway.

She had rings on both pinky toes, an ankle bracelet containing a tiny red heart, and smooth tan legs shaped to perfection by nature. The cotton shorts looked like boys' underwear, but both her brothers were much too thin to have worn them. Her belly button peeked over the waist of the pants. Her midriff was as tan as her legs and flat. The undershirt barely covered her breasts, and she wore a golden cross round her neck.

Sade smirked. I may have found my virgin, he thought.

Her hands rubbed her upper arms seeking to find some warmth in the chilly house. When she passed by him he could smell a mixture of lavender and vanilla. She wore her hair atop her head, the large hairpins clutching big chunks of her thick hair.

She walked on to a far door in the living room and stopped. She shivered, but not with cold. No, he saw her look about the room sensing that someone watched. She wavered wondering whether she should go on or rush back to the safety of her bed. Her shoulders shrugged and she made her choice, opening the door in front of her.

He moved stealthily across the floor of the living room and reached the open doorway within seconds. He saw the girl putting a small iron teapot on the stove. Well-used, he assumed, from its heavily blackened bottom.

The girl rummaged through one of the closets not

knowing that Sade had moved into the kitchen and was closing in on his victim. She stood on tiptoe when one of his hands covered her mouth and the other grabbed her about the waist. She kicked backward with her feet, but she wore no shoes and he barely felt the force. She used her elbows and attempted to bite Sade's fingers, but he gripped her so hard that she stopped fighting and tried to catch her breath.

"I once knew a girl as young as you. She called me Uncle and teased me with her flesh. Like you her skin was smooth, unblemished, and I marred her skin with my lust. Lust for blood. And now she betrays me in my dreams."

The girl remained still, listening to her captor's words.

He lowered his lips to her ear. "Will you betray me too? You don't even know me. You've never seen my face. Never listened to stories I've had to tell or tolerated my fits of anger. For you I'm a shadow that's taken on weight. A spirit come to haunt you unto death."

She began fighting again, using her hands to rip at his strong fingers, which covered her mouth.

He felt her tears flow onto his fingers. "My little girl can't come back. I forbid it. I love her too much to allow her back into my life."

He heard her try to scream, try to call for help, but the sounds were all muffled by his hand. His forearm lay across her right breast feeling the jiggle of the baby fat and the hardening tip of a woman. He dug his fingernails into her naked midriff and smelled the blood coming from her injured flesh.

"Human blood," he muttered, savoring the almost forgotten scent. "I'm famished, child." He rested his cheek against hers. "Do I smell fetid to you? Why shouldn't I since I've been dead for centuries? You're in the arms of a historical figure, *ma beauté*. I could whisper my name to you, but you wouldn't believe."

"Pappa!"

Sade sighed, recognizing the voice of a small boy behind him.

"I was hoping to spend more time luxuriating in your beauty and blood, but your brother most cruelly cuts our time together short."

Sade dug his teeth into her neck and heard only the whimpering sounds of a girl fighting for life. He no longer heard her brother, and would swiftly deal with the father when he intruded.

The blood was thick, creamy, and salty. The smell sweet, bearing the mark of health. The more blood rolled down his gullet, the heavier the girl became, until she limply rested in his arms. Her body fell to the floor, specks of red marring the white tiles of the kitchen. He squatted and pulled out all her hairpins, gathering her hair into his hands, pouring the strands over her shoulders.

"*Ma beauté*, our time was too short. I could have made love to you and taken you in tenderness, but your father would not have allowed that. If only you also could have shared the pleasure."

He shook his head and stood. In the living room he heard both boys trying to wake their father. When he reached the father's bedroom, he watched as a drunk swatted at his children, a bottle of liquor lying at the foot of the bed. Sensing Sade's presence, the boys quieted and stared with rounded eyes, giving their father time to fall back into his fitful snoring.

"If you tell no one about me, I will not come back for you. Do you understand?"

The two little heads nodded.

"Go back to bed."

The boys looked at each other.

"Quick, or I'll eat you both up."

The boys jumped out of their father's bed, and ran past Sade to their room, where each climbed into his own bed.

Sade felt confident that because of the dark and his disheveled condition, the boys would be unable to describe him, but to make sure he added, "Remember, if either of you tell I will come back and devour the both of you."

The boys pulled the covers over their heads, folding their bodies into little balls.

Sade smiled and returned to the kitchen to take the body with him. He would bury her deep in the wood. A runaway, not uncommon in this area of the country where the thrills of the city beckon the young.

He left by the rear door, leaving the golden retriever scratching at the front door.

Chapter Six

An old woman rocked in her chair, her feet rested upon a pile of animal furs. Her hands, limp, dangled off the edge of the chair's arms.

Her granddaughter brought her blankets to warm her bones and light broths to feed her empty stomach. When she could no longer sit, her granddaughter helped lift her from the rocking chair and aided in the long walk to bed. The old woman had always kept her altar beside the bed decorated with beads, candles, carved wooden saints, and brightly colored cloths in which to mix her gris-gris. Her granddaughter stitched poppets, little dolls in which she placed her wishes, but the old woman didn't bother with such images. Her power was greater than that.

But now they sat together in front of the window watching the decorative railing outside the window slowly rust. The orange color spreading a little more each day, the paint peeling into chips. On the windowsill herbs grew in planters. Herbs to cure. Herbs to banish. Herbs to find love. Herbs to seek vengeance.

Centuries old, Marie Laveau knew every herb that existed and did not fear using them. Sometimes the rich smells of the herbs caught in her throat and caused her to cough. Her body too was vulnerable to the power of the herbs. But she knew how to use them for protection and longevity.

She felt a slight breeze as her granddaughter fanned her with the Indian peacock feathers. The warm night drifted through the open window causing more discomfort for her granddaughter than for her, she knew. She waved a hand indicating that she did not need the fan.

"But Grandmother, the heat is intolerable tonight."

"For you. My cold body craves the warmth of this world. The other world that awaits me will freeze my flesh later."

She feared she had cheated the other world for too long. Her cramps and aches were constant. Her flesh, no longer elastic, felt heavy. Her mind traveled back in time too often. And those that she remembered were all gone. All but one.

"Grandmother, I will go to France soon. You will need someone to care for you."

"No," Marie Laveau said. "I will sleep in this chair. And as for food, I can still walk to the kitchen. I need very little nourishment to keep me alive. There's a small boy living across the street. I will have him run minor errands for me. Most of the time I shall be with you in spirit."

"But what if you should fall?"

Marie laughed. "If I fall I will get up. I always have."

The granddaughter nodded and used the Indian peacock feathers to dry her own wet brow.

Chapter Seven

Marie, Sade's mother-in-law, hadn't seen him since they had returned from the States. He seemed to have lost interest in settling his differences with her. She went about doing as she pleased, and even considered making another attempt at creating her own den of vampires. Sade had always been so touchy about that. He allowed himself to create and destroy, but limited others to only destruction.

"Does Madame wish to try that on?"

Marie looked down at her hands and saw that she was clutching a black beaded dress. A dress that was similar to the one she had worn to her younger daughter's funeral.

"No, I have no use for black anymore. My mourning days are over."

The shopkeeper nodded and offered to show Marie another garment.

"Ah, something in bright red, maybe a sash that would drape from one hip and a deep slit on the other side of the dress. You know, bordello-style." She grinned.

"We have some very sexy dresses, madame, but none in red. It is simply not the color of the season I'm afraid."

"Red is for every season, young lady. It goes well with my dark hair and ivory skin."

"An order could be placed. . . ."

Marie waved a hand at the shopkeeper.

"No, I need immediate gratification. I need a red dress for tonight. Nothing else will do. I'm sorry, I'll have to try your competition down the block."

"I hope she'll be able to help, madame, but I wouldn't count on it." The shopkeeper walked away from Marie and cozied up to another customer who looked more amenable.

"Hmmff," Marie loudly pronounced as she went for the door.

"Maîtresse!" shouted the tall man she encountered.

She could tell that he didn't know whether to kneel or run.

"Monsieur Playa, how wonderful to see you." She had seen him two nights ago naked and begging for more lashes. "Are you buying a present for someone special?"

He looked at the shopkeeper, but she was busy selling a stiff cocktail dress in a horrid shade of chartreuse.

"I'm buying something for you, maîtresse," he said in a soft whisper.

"You needn't bother. Men are so poor at guessing women's sizes."

"No, maîtresse, it is not for you to wear." He winked.

"Oh, I should tell you that I prefer you in red."

"But you've never seen me in red."

"I envision you in red all the time in my mind. The material must be red."

"Yes, maîtresse." He nearly bowed in submission to her

request; however, the sound of the cash register reminded him of where he was.

"Good," she said, casting a nasty look over her shoulder at the shopkeeper.

Ah, to you I will say mama,
This which causes my torment!
Dad wants that I reason,
Like a big person,
Me, I say that sweets
Are valued better than reason.

—French Nursery Rhyme

Chapter Eight

"I am angry with you, Uncle." The little girl folded her arms across her chest and pushed her bottom lip forward. She stood tall and confrontational.

"My, my! What have I done now to make you look so ugly?"

She dropped her arms to her sides and loudly protested.

"I am pretty. No—beautiful. You have told me this yourself, Uncle."

"Yes, but I've never said beautiful when you were cross."

The little girl's foot scuffed the floor like a raging bull and she placed her hands on her waist.

"I am always beautiful—even when I am cross. You have taught me not to lie, but that is what you are doing now."

Sade squatted down to look into her young eyes.

"Liliana, you are right. You always are beautiful even when you engage in food fights with your cousins."

"Then I am only dirty and that can be washed off quickly," she said proudly.

Sade stood. "Now that we've settled that, shall we go for a walk in the garden?"

Again she folded her arms across her chest but this time, too conscious of how she looked, she did not pout her lower lip.

"Uncle, I want an explanation."

"I will gladly explain if you tell me what I should be explaining."

She lifted one hand and beckoned him closer with her small index finger. Sade responded by leaning over and placing his ear near her lips.

"Where is my body?" she asked.

Sade immediately stood straight and took a small step away from the child. She cocked her head waiting for an answer.

"Liliana, you chide me. That is most cruel."

"I only ask a simple question. You certainly should be able to tell me the answer."

"You are not here with me, Liliana."

She looked down at her hands, feet, and body.

"I seem to be here, Uncle." She offered her hands to Sade. "Touch my fingers and palms and you will see that I am real."

"You're no longer a little girl, Liliana. You are old and your small body is only a trick."

"Uncle, of course I'm here. Why are you being so cruel?"

"If you are here in your body, then why ask me where your body is?"

Panic caused her features to crinkle into a frown. "I'm so confused, Uncle."

"Someone is playing with the two of us, Liliana."

"It's not a very nice game," she said, her curls wriggling about her face.

"Who are you?" Sade shouted at the empty room. "I want to see you."

He heard his niece sob. He looked down at her and saw that her body faded in and out. She wanted to grab onto him for protection, but every time she tried she would nearly vanish.

"Leave my niece alone. If you have a vendetta with me, then settle it now and confront me. Let the child rest in peace."

"Uncle," Liliana cried. Tears marred her perfect features and her eyes looked swollen and red.

"She has cried enough. For centuries she has begged for peace. Let her have it now."

"I'll never rest, Uncle. We are not meant to have peace. We must pay for the lives we've stolen and the pain we've caused."

Sade dropped to his knees. "I never meant you to wail in fright or wander the earth sleepless. I only . . ."

"What did you want for me, Uncle?"

"God forgive me."

Chapter Nine

Sade awoke under the roof of a shrine dedicated to Christ. Rain poured down in front of him causing puddles to form miniature lakes that softened the soil and drove the earthworms to the surface. He reached behind and felt the cross that towered over him. He lay back against the cross.

"Tell me, Lord, what purpose do I serve besides my enjoying my own hedonistic pleasures? I took a young girl to be mine. A sin in many ways, I know, but she was such a joy to see, hear, touch. Now you torture me with her image. Why?"

Sade stood and cowered under the arch of the shrine avoiding the torrents of rain.

"Silent, eh? As you wish, but don't expect me to forgive you for this."

He knew he was just outside a small French town in which he could acquire a car to take him back to Paris.

Did he want to go? He stepped forward into a puddle that soaked his feet and splashed onto his trousers.

Looking about him, he noticed an abandoned cemetery only a few feet away.

"Who here among the dead have I met before? How many may have quenched my hunger? I've passed this way many times and only stopped briefly to satisfy my hunger for blood. I now address the women, the men who met me unexpectedly in the night. Do any of you want revenge? Come forth, don't hide." His voice rose into a yell.

He walked into the cemetery and looked at the names on the tombstones.

"Ah, Evelyn Montclair, have we met before? Did I put you into this grave?" He looked around at several other tombstones. "Pierre Roget and Pamela Stafford, do you remember me? Perhaps I didn't look as shoddy as I do now. You saw a gentleman instead of a tramp. Can you remember the touch of my hands on your flesh, the smell of my fetid breath, the sting of my bite?"

He waited for someone to rise out of the ground and confront him, but none did.

"You needn't fear me now. There isn't much I can do to you after I've stolen your lives."

His right foot skidded and fell deeper into the soil.

"No, no, you will not pull me down into your world. You must come up and face me here."

He looked around and saw rain pitting holes in the dirt, washing tombstones clean, and soaking the clothes he wore.

"I am drunk from virgin blood." He sat on the closest tombstone. "No one here has any power over me. And

God could care less about what I do. Only one woman would know so much about Liliana and hate me enough to use the child against me. I must go back to Paris and deal with her."

Chapter Ten

Marie fussed over her client. She didn't always get an opportunity to serve one so high up in government. She thought back to the days when Marie Antoinette and Louis XVI were on France's throne. Marie, through her husband and the money he had made, had been able to influence some of the more sensitive decisions of government. There were the balls and the dinners and the . . .

"How much do you charge, madame?"

"Oh, that can be discussed later, monsieur." She reached for his topcoat.

"No, madame, I wish to know the sum you will charge."

It was so much better to draw them into her kinky web and then state a price. By the time they'd been lashed and bled, they usually were quite amenable to any price she quoted.

"I'm sure you have a schedule to which you can refer." The man had begun to rebutton his overcoat.

"I don't. It depends on how much pleasure we share."

She smiled and stood tall, reminding him of who the dominant person was.

"That doesn't work for me, madame. If you can't quote a price, then I am leaving."

Marie stepped back several feet, pulled a thick whip from the hall tree, and snapped the whip in the air.

"Take your clothes off now, you wimp."

The silence seemed to last forever while he stared at her.

"Fool," the client murmured and started for the front door.

She snapped the whip at the door, marring the white paint.

"No one walks out on me, monsieur. I'm not playing games like some cheap whore you can pick up on the street. This is a way of life for me. It is not the money that is important." She didn't add that it was blood she most sought.

"After our time together I will pay you, madame, what I think you are worth. Is that agreeable?"

"Monsieur, I will not let you bankrupt yourself."

The client broke out into laughter.

Before he unbuttoned his topcoat he asked, "We are alone? There are no hidden cameras?"

"Again you offend me by taking me for a street whore."

"We are alone? No cameras?" he repeated.

"Let me take you on a tour of the apartment, monsieur. You will see that I am discreet. You pay me cash and I keep no paperwork." She cracked her whip one more time. "Step away from the door, monsieur, and follow me."

Chapter Eleven

The horse-drawn carriages still traveled the streets of New Orleans. The elderly woman heard the clop of the hooves passing her building. She rocked in her chair stitching together gris-gris for her granddaughter to carry on the plane. She'd miss the woman who had volunteered to conduct her grandmother's business, and wanted to be sure that she would return home safely.

Marie had burned protective herbs and mixed them with native soil to act as a magnet to bring home her granddaughter. The material she had wrapped them in was old and worn very thin, but still it served as an adequate container. The material had been part of her celebratory costume when she had been Vodou Queen in New Orleans. Her common-law husband Christophe Glapion had given her the bright red material as a gift after she bore the first of their fifteen children. She remembered him as a gentle man who did not approve of her vocation but never suggested she quit her role as Vodou Queen.

"Grandmother."

Marie Laveau smiled. She had just put in the last stitch needed.

"Come here, child. I have something for you."

The woman rushed to Marie Laveau's side and knelt to accept the gift.

"Here, take this gris-gris with you so that I am sure you will come back safely." Marie Laveau dropped the bundle into her granddaughter's hand and felt the invisible tangle of threads that connected the two women. This will surely work, she thought, my granddaughter will never be far from me.

"You must carry this with you all the time. Pin it to your bra near your heart so that I may give you courage."

"I'm already brave, Grandmother."

"You have not met him yet. Monsieur Sade is cruel and charming. He manipulates everyone. You will react no differently."

"He will suffer, Grandmother, I promise he will pay dearly."

"He already suffers, child, but has no idea that I bring him his pain. If he thinks of me at all, he thinks of a corpse rotting in the ground. I was born in seventeen-ninety-four; by now most humans would be dust."

"Not you, Grandmother. You are too powerful."

Marie Laveau sighed and pulled the cashmere shawl tighter around her body. "Someday I too will have to answer to God, but not until I've gotten my vengeance on Sade."

"I don't ever want to lose you."

"And you won't. Do you think death can steal me away from you? You and I are one. My blood runs through your veins. You are now Marie Laveau, Vodou Queen of New Orleans. Forget the name your mother called you. I will say my rosary for that little girl and burn her effigy into ash. You are Marie Laveau. When I see you I am looking into a mirror. You are me a century ago when I was beautiful."

"You still are."

"I have transferred all my beauty to you, child. Use it."

"On the man who refused eternal life to you."

Marie nodded. "Yes. On the Marquis de Sade, who taught me the pain of love and the emptiness of trust."

Are you sleeping? Are you sleeping?
Brother John, brother John?
Morning bells are ringing. Morning bells are ringing,
Ding, dong, ding. Ding, dong, ding.

—French Nursery Rhyme

Chapter Twelve

Sade could hear Liliana's voice coming from the playroom.

Frère Jacques, Frère Jacques,
Dormez-vous? Dormez-vous?
Sonnez les matines. Sonnez les matines.
Din, din, don. Din, din, don.

He peeked into the room and saw Liliana sitting on the Chinese rug with all her dolls circling her. They all had shut eyes and were attired in nightshirts.

"What are you doing, Liliana?" he asked.

"Shh! Singing my babies to sleep, Uncle. They can be very naughty at bedtime."

"You mean they don't wish to go to bed?"

She shook her head.

"Does singing a lullaby help put them to sleep?"

"Usually." She began covering each doll with a miniature blanket.

"Are they all asleep now?"

"Mmmm. I'm not sure about Michel. He often cheats. He'll open his eyes as soon as Nanny turns off the light."

"And what does he do?"

"He wakes everyone else and makes them sit on the shelves over there. Uncle, they can't be comfortable on those shelves, can they?"

"Maybe they don't mind. They may want to make Michel happy. He might not be able to sleep on the floor and the others are able to fall asleep anywhere."

"Do you think they cheat dreams that way?"

"I don't understand."

"Well, when dreams sneak about looking for sleepers, maybe they never think of approaching people who are sitting up with wide-open eyes." The child stood. "That's what we should do, Uncle."

"I don't think you'd be able to have a very good rest if you kept your eyes open."

"Are you bothered by dreams, Uncle?"

He'd fallen into this trap too many times, he realized. He tried to back out of the room, but the little girl kept walking toward him.

"Are you fleeing from me, Uncle? Don't you love me anymore?"

He wanted to turn away from her, but he couldn't. "Someone is tricking us, Liliana. Someone pushes us back in time, but we can't go back. I was greedy. Please forgive me, Liliana."

The child looked around at the room. "Aren't you here with me, Uncle?"

Sade said nothing.

"Uncle, please tell me you're with me. I don't want to

be alone." She looked behind her at the dolls lying on the floor. "They don't make good company, Uncle. They're too silent and still. Besides, they feel cold against my skin like you." She turned back toward Sade.

"I'm dead, Liliana. I've been dead most of your life."

"Then I must be dead too if I can see and hear you." A dark frown crumpled her face. "I don't want to be dead, Uncle. Not anymore."

"I can't bring you back, Liliana. I'll never allow anyone to bring you back."

Chapter Thirteen

Sade awoke feeling calm. He had made a choice and he would stand by it. If his wretched mother-in-law wanted to curse him with these nightmares, he would end her existence.

He sprinted from his casket and made preparations for his evening meal. He'd call one of the usual prostitutes who was willing to share her blood. After their visits to him, the prostitutes left weaker but still alive, and he kept a list, giving each a chance to recuperate before the next bleeding.

An hour after his feeding Sade stood in front of an apartment door. He tried the knob. No luck. He could crash in the door and probably wake everyone in the building, or he could be the gentleman and ring the bell. Splintering the door into pieces was the most appealing idea, but hardly sensible.

He gently pressed the lighted bell and waited. He wondered whether he should place his palm over the peephole in the door. However, he and Marie had parted last time on good terms and she might not know of his suspicions. She always underestimated him.

"Louis. You've been on my mind a lot lately." She stood in her doorway, her front door open wide.

"I thought you might say that." He walked past her into the apartment.

"Come in," she said. "Don't bother to ask permission. After all, we are family."

Marie closed the door and Sade heard the numerous locks being done up.

"Have many problems with burglaries?" he asked.

"Habit," she answered. "I had all those locks put on after our last misunderstanding. You remember, after you tried to destroy me."

"Not after I actually did?"

"I forgave you, Louis. Look at me. I have a much younger body. You did me a favor when you burned up my old hide."

"I didn't mean for you to come back."

"I know, Louis. I've forgiven you. Your sweet young thing, Cecelia, brought me back. She was trying to get revenge on you as I recall."

"She didn't mean to bring you back either."

"I've always been one to take advantage of a situation."

Sade lunged at Marie and tightly grasped her throat, throwing her against a wall.

"I remembered that after initially blaming God and my victims."

"Me too," she rasped. "*Victim.*"

"You were no victim, Marie. You forced me to change you into a vampire. I never wanted to have you around."

"The feeling was mutual, Louis. Could you let go of my

throat? It would make it easier for me to communicate with you. Obviously there's been some misunderstanding."

Sade poked his thumb into the center of Marie's throat causing her to have a coughing fit. He flung her to the floor and stood over her, his heel buried in her chest.

"Louis, I really don't know why you're so angry. I've been contentedly engaged in my dominatrix business and have only given you a passing thought once in a while. Although for me that was too often."

"You weren't surprised to see me."

"Louis, you frequently show up unannounced. By now I accept that irritating quality of yours."

"I'm not surprised you would seek to torture me, but I wouldn't have expected you to use Liliana."

"Liliana is gone. There is no way I would ever hurt the child. You were the one to ruin her life."

"You haven't tried to bring Liliana back?"

"What are you saying?" Her face froze with fear.

Sade eased off her chest, settling his foot back on the marble floor. "You did love the child."

Marie rose to her feet. "Someone is trying to bring her back?"

Sade turned away and walked to the window overlooking the busy avenue. He felt Marie's hand shake the sleeve of his shirt.

"What has happened, Louis?"

"I've been dreaming."

"Daydreams?"

"No, dreams come to me when I sleep."

"Impossible, Louis. We can't dream. We fall into the sleep of death. There's nothing but silence. Our bodies spoil while we sleep and refresh when it is time to wake."

"I am dreaming of Liliana. I think someone has reached her spirit, forcing her to link with me. She believes she's a child again and she takes a childlike shape."

"Is she the only person in your dreams?"

"The only person I can see. But we both feel someone watching us."

"How long has this been going on?"

"Over three months."

"Why didn't you come here sooner?"

Sade smiled and turned to Marie. "I didn't want to believe it was you. I blamed God and my victims but not you. You should have been the first one I suspected."

"You didn't suspect me because I love Liliana. If I were to use someone, it would be that foolish girl of yours, Cecelia. A dumb tramp. I don't even know how to communicate with the spirits. Did you think I sit around in front of a crystal ball communing with spirits and watching everything you do? Your life doesn't interest me."

"It did when you were human."

"That's when you took up with my daughters. They're out of your reach now."

"Liliana isn't. We're being made to live together when I'm not able to protect myself."

"You've made so many enemies that we couldn't even draw up a list of possible people."

Marie walked back and forth across her living room.

"Louis, did you keep any part of Liliana's body?"

"No, I took back my ring from her finger. That's all. I left her flesh for those monsters and hate myself for that."

"Could it be your own guilt playing games with your mind?"

"No, Marie. Someone out there is controlling us."

"Sleep here tonight and I'll watch over you."

Sade's eyes narrowed.

"Oh, Louis, I'm not going to stake you. If I did, I wouldn't be able to help Liliana."

"I'll consider your offer, Marie."

"Louis Sade, are you going to allow someone to torture your own . . ."

"Don't, Marie. Only you and I know fully what Liliana meant to me. Don't utter the words lest someone should hear."

"There's no one else here, Louis."

"We can't be sure."

"Do you feel another's presence?"

Sade flopped into a leather chair and raised his feet up on a matching ottoman. He sat silent. Not even Marie broke the quiet of the room.

"I don't know. There is an aching in my heart that blocks my feelings for everything and everyone else. Liliana is always with me. When I'm awake she cannot talk to me, but she's attached to me now. Where I go she must go."

He sat pensively looking far into the past and seeing events he would rather forget. Blood stained every vision.

"I carry Liliana's guilt." He laughed. "I suddenly know what guilt is and I don't like it. I want my life back. I want the pleasures that enabled me to survive all these years without going insane."

"I can help you get your life back, Louis. Trust me."

"You, Marie, I will never trust. I severed your head from your shoulders and burned your flesh. I foolishly kept your skull at my feet when I rested until that brainless Cecelia saw fit to rob me of it. If I allowed you to watch me in my sleep, would I awake in my body or would I wake to the smell of my own burning flesh?"

"Tempting." Her eyes glittered with glee. "But if I destroy you, how do I help Liliana? You should trust my love for my granddaughter."

On the bridge of Avignon
They are dancing, they are dancing,
On the bridge of Avignon
They are dancing all around.
The pretty dames go this way
And then again go that way
On the bridge of Avignon
They are dancing all around.

—French Nursery Rhyme

Chapter Fourteen

Masked women grabbed at Sade attempting to pull him into a dance. He politely bowed, but continued to move down the path to the bridge. He passed bushes alive with panting breaths and drunken giggles. A girl just beginning her puberty smiled at him and bared a shapely ankle. Her mask appeared to be a cross between Medusa and Helen of Troy, causing fear but also enticing.

He stopped, glancing from the girl to the bridge where several nobles were carousing with naked women. Women in masks, high-born women who believed they would never be recognized in the midst of all the debauchery. Experienced women who knew how to touch and taste a lover. The men were partially dressed with torn shirts and breeches that were lowered to their thighs. Men who, although spent, were willing to be coaxed into another round.

But Sade couldn't help but look back at the girl, dressed in a yellow gown that tightly closed around her breasts, pushing her small mounds to peek out. Her hands fluttered through the folds of her skirt in time to a distant tune. Her small feet tapped out the rhythm while her body bounced with the excitement of the music.

Too young, he thought, and glanced back to the bridge. Some of the men had stumbled on their breeches and lay in a drunken heap on the wooden boards of the bridge. The women teased, spreading their legs over the men, taunting them with the sight and smell.

A midget grabbed his hands and pulled him toward a gazebo filled with flowers, wine, and food. He picked the midget up and danced around in a circle passing very close to the girl, who smelled of strawberries and blueberries. His mouth watered. The midget's mask appeared before his eyes. A sad mask with tiny teardrops painted in black down the cheeks of the white face. The midget threw her arms about his neck and in opposition to the mask, laughed merrily.

He looked for the girl. She remained where he had first seen her, still moving to the music.

"So where, my little friend, are the musicians?" he asked the midget.

A small chubby hand pointed beyond the girl.

"Ah, perhaps I should seek them out."

He placed the midget back on the path and moved toward the music, toward the girl. When he could almost touch her, she ran ahead until hidden by a grove of trees. And then he saw the musicians dressed in fancy clothes and with somber faces. They didn't seem to notice the guests. They played on as if playing for themselves.

He looked over his shoulder at the bridge. The men

looked worn out and the women old. He decided to check out the grove.

He walked, but the grove never got nearer.

"Miss," he called, "I need to speak to you. Please come out. Don't be frightened of me. I just want to see you one more time before I must leave."

Her mask popped out from behind a tree. The snakes making up her hair almost appeared to be moving, but then he thought it might only be the sway of her body that caused the illusion.

"Come out and introduce yourself."

She shook her head no, and Sade immediately fell victim to her.

"I cannot let you get away without at least a brief introduction. How will I know you next time?"

She stepped out from behind the tree and folded her hands in front of her, lowering her head shyly.

He felt his penis swell and his breeches clung to its outline. He smiled to himself, glad that she could see.

"I'm coming closer. Please don't run away again."

His steps were slow and small. He didn't want to frighten her.

"How do you come to be here, mademoiselle?"

She raised an index finger to the lips painted onto the mask.

"Do you mean to keep that secret?" he asked.

He was hungry for this girl/woman. Yes, she was young, but her body was ripe. He could imagine her, the slick walls of her vagina throbbing with desire for him and her nipples aching for his hands.

He reached for her hands and noticed how small they

were and that they were cold. She giggled, and the sound seemed familiar. He reached for her mask, but she pushed his hand away.

"Why can't I see your face? Do I already know you?"

The young woman nodded.

"Give me a name. Give me at least a hint."

The familiar giggle sent a chill up his spine.

Her hands reached up to grab each side of the mask. Quickly she pulled the mask from her face.

"Boo," she shouted, whipping the mask off.

Chapter Fifteen

"Louis. Louis. Don't let go of her, please." Marie's voice came from far away. She asked for wishes that could not be fulfilled. He couldn't stop Liliana from going. He found that he didn't want to.

He opened his eyes. Marie stood above him, her mouth gaping open and her eyes filled with misery.

"You saw her again, didn't you?" she asked.

"Liliana was slightly older and she was hiding from me."

"Well, that doesn't surprise me. What did she want?"

"To tease."

"Your body . . ."

"What?"

"You were jerking about as if you were a puppet. You didn't seem to be in charge of your own movements."

"I'm sure I wasn't."

"While you sleep someone is able to control your soul. Whoever it is probably has full control over Liliana. You can't rest until we've found out who this person is. Don't you realize that not only you are at risk, but also your . . ."

Sade sat up quickly. "No, Marie, don't preach to me." He stood. "Did you see anything else?"

"Your flesh went slack, only it didn't decay. There was the smell of incense and herbs. When I leaned closer to you I sensed the odor arising from your body. Louis, this frightens me. Who would be able to gain such control over you?"

"No one."

"Liar! I watched you drift off into death, but something stopped the full transition. Your skin is grayer than it was because it can't refresh itself."

Sade walked to the front door. "I'm hungry, Marie. I must feed."

"Blood can do just so much for you. You need death to renew your flesh and organs."

"I carry death wherever I go, Marie."

"No. Whoever is doing this takes over your body and prevents death from revitalizing you."

"My body screams for blood. I may need to kill tonight."

"What if you need to kill every night? You become a danger to all vampires. Too many bodies . . ."

"Shut up!" He made an effort to calm his temper. "I will be careful. I'll not drink my fill. And yes, Marie, I can control myself enough to do that. It is when I sleep that I lose control."

"Don't sleep until you know you are free of this burden."

Sade leaned against the wall and rested his head in his hands.

"I can watch over you," Marie offered.

"And do what? Prevent my muscles from going into spasms? How would you attempt that?"

"I'd sit on you if I had to. If I could protect my granddaughter from you."

Sade dropped his hands by his sides. "Only I can save Liliana."

"If you walk out of here, I'll still remember what I saw and do what I can to protect Liliana."

"Do that, Marie, but don't get in my way."

Chapter Sixteen

The announcement had just been made that they were about to land in Paris. The granddaughter put away all the papers she had been reading. Stories about her grandmother's affair with the Marquis de Sade. Her grandfather Glapion had been a patient man. He watched his common-law wife fall deeper and deeper in love with a shadow of a man. A vampire.

Marie Laveau's own son, Jacques, introduced the Marquis de Sade to his mother when he returned from Paris. Sade had traveled with Jacques. Marie Laveau suspected that her son was intoxicated by the fast life Sade lived. She wanted to talk to the man who had so much control over her son. Jacques proudly brought his friend home thinking that the family would be impressed by the sophisticated Frenchman.

"No Cajun-pidgin language. Monsieur Sade speaks the true French, Mama. He has been living in Paris, dining at the finest restaurants, and meeting the most beautiful and exotic women."

"And you, Jacques, have you been hanging on to your new friend, hoping his luck would rub off on you?"

"Mama, it is not luck he possesses. No, he is a true noble gentleman. He lives in a palace." Jacques took a moment to think. "Perhaps not a palace, but certainly a great house bigger than anything you've seen here in New Orleans. A mansion with gardens and fountains. One can't see to the end of his property."

"And because of that you think he is great."

"Wait, wait until you meet him, Mama. You will recognize his powers."

And Marie Laveau fell under the Marquis de Sade's spell. A spell stronger than anything Marie Laveau had ever created. Grandfather Glapion watched and waited. It must have been difficult to watch one's own woman fleeing into the arms of so magical a figure.

Did her grandfather believe his common-law wife would return to him, or had he given up and abandoned any thought of a fight? There were nights her grandfather spent alone watching over the children that were still left in the house, feeding them, and consoling them. "Mother needs to be away for a while, but she misses each of you and asks about you every day."

But in her journal Marie Laveau admits her sight narrowed down to only one man. A man who was not really a man but a spirit living in two worlds, embracing two extremes, life and death.

Ashamed at seeing his father shoved to the side, Jacques attempted to talk his mother into returning to Grandfather Glapion.

Marie Laveau wrote about the tears she shed when she realized how she had ostracized the man who loved her. The vampire fucked her but never made love to her. Sade educated her in the fine art of cooking, and his stories were so real. He had lived and had breathed the history he had spoken about. He knew the royals, the master of the guillotine, the charms of famous paramours, and the intrigue of despots. Most of all he talked about eternal existence, the body never growing older but stronger.

"And what of his soul?" Grandfather Glapion had asked.

"What of his soul, Christopher?"

"Does it grow blacker day by day? What sins has he committed against God, Marie? Can he go to Mass with you?"

"I've never asked him to, Christopher. I always return here on Sundays and go with my family."

"You don't leave sin behind in that decrepit mansion when you leave him. Whatever you do with him you take with you on your soul. You expose your children to all the temptations you have given into."

"No, Christopher, that is not true. I keep my life with Sade separate. The only child that has met Sade is Jacques, and he was the one who introduced me. . . ."

"And how do you think Jacques feels? Now you are never home and the other children know why."

"You have never once told me what to do with my life. Now that is to change?"

Her grandfather remained silent and allowed his beloved to continue her sham of a family.

But the vampire eventually became tired of Marie Laveau. Her tears and pleading could not reach his cold heart. She begged at least to share in eternal life. Her beauty was important to her and she had so many experiences yet to be fulfilled.

Grandfather Glapion had to guide his common-law wife home. She spoke to no one for three months. She sat in her room oblivious of the children. Jacques deprecated Sade. "A man interested in only himself. He has no soul. He isn't even a man. He left you sitting in that house alone and unprotected. If Father hadn't . . ."

But she waved him away and lifted the hair from her old wooden box. The vampire's hair. Hair she had collected while he slept because she was a Vodou Queen and would someday have her revenge.

Chapter Seventeen

Sade drove the ten miles from the Béziers airport to La Cité d'Agde. He didn't stay long in the walled city since his final destination was Cap d'Agde, the Naturalist Quarter. Some came here to enjoy the eight miles of beaches and the warm weather. Others, like Sade, came to enjoy the swinging lifestyle.

He knew there were four swinger clubs: Le Glamour, Le Loft, Le Pharon, and Nat Hammam—a sauna club. Sade had been to three of the four and intended to escape his depression by going to the fourth.

First he needed to find a companion since the clubs allowed entrance only to couples. He walked the streets viewing the many fetish clothing stores hoping that a customer would catch his eye. Even though the two major languages spoken were French and German, there were many English tourists, who tired of the dark, damp days of the British Isles and came here for holiday. Many of the people were middle-class; no jet-setters, but Sade wanted to go slumming.

This night he found few beauties shopping and parading the streets. He could call a particularly sexy prostitute that he had used before, but somehow the idea of paying didn't appeal to him tonight.

Out of boredom he walked into one of the S/M clothing stores. He watched several women and men try on knee-high boots, latex suits that covered the wearer from neck to toe, and belts and straps that didn't seem to have a reason to be worn since they covered none of the genitals but instead emphasized breasts and penises.

"May I help you?"

He looked to his right and saw a middle-aged woman with dyed black hair and wearing enough makeup to last a week without touch-up.

"You work here?" he asked.

"Sometimes," she said.

"I take it tonight is one of those sometimes."

"No."

Sade's eyebrows rose.

"I just want to help you," she said.

"Fine, do you have any suggestions, madame?"

"Lots, but none of them are decent."

Sade looked around the store. "I suppose if I wanted decent, I wouldn't have come in here."

The woman smiled.

"Again let me ask, do you have any suggestions?"

She wore a deep green velvet cape that she hugged close to her body. At her throat she wore a silver and gold fertility-goddess pin. She poked one hand out of the cape, undid the clasp, and slowly let the cape fall away from her body.

She had heavy breasts that were wrapped in leather bindings that went over her shoulder. Her breasts protruded like delectable offerings. Her waist was tiny, and Sade suspected that she had removed a rib or two to make it so small. Her hips bloomed out, the buttocks were lifted by the same type of leather bindings that held her breasts, and her belly was surprisingly flat with only a hint of a scar cutting across the surface of the skin. He noticed that the leather bindings continued down her thighs, circling her knees, and ended wrapped around shapely ankles. Manolo Blahnick heels heightened her five-six figure.

"I see you could be of help, madame."

"I'm one of the best salespeople here."

"Now that you've sold the merchandise to me, shall we go?"

"I'm not a prostitute. I don't intend to be paid for tonight. I want to make that clear."

"Could I have thought anything else about you, madame?"

He quickly moved to the door and reached for the handle, but the woman called him back.

"Where are we going, monsieur? I don't accept cash, but I want to be sure that I have fun wherever I go."

"Ah, I thought you were too easy. There's a club that I've yet to try and I thought . . ."

"Yes, I love all the clubs. Would you believe some ignorant fool wanted to take me to an empty beach? Me looking the way I do? The fool didn't know enough to show me off."

"Perhaps he wanted to keep you all to himself, madame."

"One-on-one's far too boring. I need crowds. Not knowing who is touching me or inside me is part of the excitement."

"Then you'll have a good time tonight."

He began to move toward the door again, but was stopped by her fingernails sinking into the flesh of his forearms.

"Tonight I'm Lizzie, and you, monsieur?"

"Louis. Louis, like I am every night."

Lizzie seemed to know everyone inside the club. Some knew her by different names, but still she had many acquaintances.

"Madame, I see you have been here many times."

"Why not? I live here in Cap d'Agde. I'm no tourist. I look for action." She rubbed her breast against Sade's arm and pressed his hand into her pubic hair.

Sade checked out the room, and was disappointed to see so many cubicles. Little holes were cut out in most of the walls where "tourists" kneeled to get a preview of what the evening could bring. He preferred the open rooms where there was no slinking about for a secret look.

"I'm not sure this place will meet my needs, madame."

"You have me. What more could you want, monsieur?"

"A whipping post."

Chapter Eighteen

Lizzie proved to be not as much fun as she had promised. Immediately upon hearing the words "whipping post" she bolted, leaving Sade to explore on his own. He didn't mind since that gave him far more freedom and lots of choices. However, he felt a certain disappointment in Lizzie. She looked so ripe for the role he'd had in mind for her.

He had paid two hundred dollars to get in, and still carried around his token for a "free" drink. He wondered whether he should have stayed in the city instead of traveling out to the cape. He had spent many exciting nights at Le Feeling located on the embankment of the Quai des Dames. The nightclub and playroom were cut into the rock underneath one of the city squares. An interesting location, but still not what he looked for tonight.

The Chateau, contained in a country house, was much more to his liking. Sadomasochistic equipment abounded in this club. Stocks, pillories, and huge X-shaped whipping frames covered the first floor—

although he found the house dominatrices lacking in strength and beauty.

"You're marked, monsieur."

He turned to see a small woman dressed in leather. Various tattoos marked her cheeks and her eyebrows had been thinned far too much.

"I see that you are trapped, monsieur. Many threads hold you in place." Her black-painted fingernails rested on her deep red lips. "You walk alone and go where you please but you're not free."

He reached out to touch her, but she cringed away from him, spreading her hands in front of her.

"You never sleep anymore. Not true sleep. You have strong ties to the spirit world. Ties of love, yes, but also bindings that you must break."

She ran her fingers through her strawberry-blond hair pulling the curls back behind her ears.

"I can smell the curse that's on you. I hear the spirit that calls to you."

"What do you know about me?"

"Only what I see in front of me. A man who is not a man. A ghost who is bound to the earth. A father rejecting his own child."

Sade grabbed her arms before she could move away.

"Tell me how you know all this."

Her eyes widened and she let out a scream. He let her go and watched as she ran to the back of the club. Afraid that she had caused too much of a scene, Sade worked his way toward the exit.

There was once a flower
It opens a little, then a lot
A butterfly comes and rests on the flower
Mmmm, how nice that smells
The butterfly flies away out of sight
The flower closes up, withers and disappears.

—French Nursery Rhyme

Chapter Nineteen

Sade traveled down an old dirt road wondering where he was headed. The trees leaned over the road, giving shade from the sun. Once in a while the sun peeked through and Sade felt searing pain pass down his flesh. He didn't know why he felt especially vulnerable to the sun today. Usually he could take limited walks during the day. He couldn't remember how long he had been on the road. He judged it to be midday. Perhaps he had started at dawn, but why would he have done that?

He recalled fleeing the club after meeting . . . a gypsy? A witch? She knew something and he had wanted to know what it was. Or *had* he wanted to know?

The dirt from the road scuffed his shoes and the pebbles made walking unsteady. He thought about stopping, but he knew he was heading someplace special. He had to keep his appointment with someone. Why couldn't he remember with whom?

A bend in the road led him to a cemetery. He saw a

young woman dressed in black with flowers in her hands. Mixed flowers, wildflowers. He turned into the cemetery to have a closer look and recognized his niece, Liliana. He quickened his step in anticipation of seeing her up close and talking to her. He even tried calling to her, but she kept moving along the path.

All the graves looked fresh in this cemetery, and the stones and monuments were new. Most graves had bushels of flowers and portraits of those buried here.

"Liliana," he called, but she didn't turn around; she kept walking.

Finally she stopped at a huge weeping angel frozen in a crouch by the artist who had carved it. The grave had new sod and an iron fence separating it from the rest.

Liliana placed the flowers at the foot of the angel and knelt, crossing herself swiftly.

"Liliana, who is buried here?" He didn't recognize the monument or the layout of the cemetery. He hadn't been here before. Or had he?

Liliana took a hanky from her purse and dabbed at her eyes. He could hear her quiet sobs. He wondered who could be buried inside this elaborate grave. The marble used for the angel was priceless. The deceased had to be wealthy. He tried to make out an inscription on the pedestal, but he needed to move closer to read it.

"Liliana, is this your mother's grave?" he asked. He had never bothered to visit his wife's sister's grave after attending her funeral. Their time together had been tumultuous and he didn't need to be reminded of it.

The flowers placed on the grave by Liliana began to separate one from the other, until several actually blew away in the wind. What wind? he wondered, sensing only stillness.

Stillness in a cemetery. Liliana quietly praying. The images couldn't be real. His death sleep played tricks on him again.

He wanted to turn away and go back down to the road, but he couldn't. Forward he had to go. He stepped over the fence and felt his shoes sink into the soft sod.

"Uncle."

Liliana stood now and her right hand pointed at something inscribed on the pedestal.

Rest in peace our little angel, Liliana

She had no grave. She had never been buried.

"Is this what you want, Liliana? Do you want a monument to mark the time you spent on this earth?"

"I want a home," she said. "I want a place to go that is all mine."

"I will give that to you if it means that you will then be able to rest."

The remaining flowers wilted and quickly turned to dust. The mournful angel cracked into two halves and toppled onto the ground. The iron gate rusted and fell into pieces.

"Can you put it all back together, Uncle?"

"No, but I can build a bigger and better monument to you and I can place it on a high hill so that everyone can see my love for you."

"And will the hill erode, Uncle?"

"It will last forever for I'll replenish it daily."

"And what will you use to keep the hill solid?"

"The best French soil I can find."
"Will you do this with your own hands?"
"If that is what you want."
She shook her head.
"I want life back."

Chapter Twenty

Sade woke swearing. Someone tricked him over and over again. No matter how hard he tried to avoid the pain, he kept charging into the hope, into the dream.

He found himself lying on a cement floor in the basement of a church. Overused religious articles surrounded him. Most had heavy blankets of dust. Smoothed-out priest's garments lay over a wooden bench waiting for the next Mass.

Sade lifted himself off the floor, but almost fell back when a sudden weakness took hold of him. His body had lost weight and his dry skin felt tight. He couldn't maintain his existence if the dreams continued. He brushed a hand through his white hair, and realized a clump of hair had fallen to the floor.

"Liliana, we must help each other. Neither of us can live an eternity like this. It's not enough if only one of us fights. We must both work toward squashing this curse."

He wondered why anyone would want to harm Liliana.

Were they so desperate to reach him that an innocent would be made to suffer?

He heard a door open and close. Footsteps echoed inside the basement. Finally he saw a male adolescent's shoe touch the floor. The boy, dressed in altar-boy clothes, hadn't noticed Sade as yet. Sade stood still. And the boy robotically headed for the priest's garments.

Does innocence matter when one is driven by hunger or revenge? Sade wondered.

He answered his own question by snatching the boy into his arms. The child made the softest of sounds before Sade bled him to death.

Chapter Twenty-one

Marie Laveau sank back into her rocking chair absorbing the spirit of the dying boy. She gripped her hands tight holding on to his soul. She rocked herself to the rhythm of his dying heart. Breathing in the stale New Orleans air, she caught the smell of feces and urine. The boy's body was done with its work. His spirit, however, was hers. Another soul to feed her revenge. Another child lost to Sade's appetite.

"Innocence. You fool, there is nothing innocent in this world," she grumbled. She brought her fists to her open mouth and swallowed the boy's soul.

Each murder Sade committed bound him closer to her as a puppet.

"Soon, Sade, even when awake you won't be able to separate the spirit world from your everyday world. The god Legba will blur your vision and welcome you into the crossroads. His giant erect penis will be buried deep inside Liliana and you, Sade, will watch as they fornicate."

The sweltering heat drenched Marie Laveau's flesh. Her swollen ankles hurt and her fingernails had begun to rot. One or two fingernails had already fallen off. She had very little time left. Age would win out over all the talismans and potions she could ever use. She looked to the corners of the room where ginger root soaked in sweet oil lay rotting like her. The power of the blackberry tea and powdered cat's eye that she drank every day no longer invigorated her the way it used to. Her swollen knuckles hurt all the time, and her ankles throbbed with water pressure from her ailing kidneys. The vertebrae of her spine had deteriorated to the point where her shoulders remained raised all the time.

Marie Laveau couldn't fight God. God's first children, the Twins Marasa, had to die. God granted them no special favor, so why should He grant more than a reprieve to Marie Laveau?

Marie Laveau turned toward the terrarium on the table next to her. Inside, her pygmy rattlesnake lay still. Only a few inches long, the snake was difficult to see among the miniature brush. The clear scales over its eyes made the snake always look alert. A grandson had found the snake in the swamp and had brought it to her as a playmate for her black rat snake.

"Playmate? Snakes are loners, boy, and this one I wouldn't let wander about the house freely."

"The snake is but an infant, Grandma."

"No, boy, I think it is full grown." And so it was. She had had the snake for three years now and it never grew any longer. Certainly she had fed the snake enough live mice to know that it wasn't malnourished. Strange, she thought, how she had never gotten around to naming the snake. Maybe it didn't want a name. Maybe it refused to introduce itself because it longed for the swamps.

Her black rat snake seemed to announce who it was immediately. The first place it made home was Marie Laveau's old hope chest, hence the name Hope. When the snake was young it had had grayish color with dark blotches. Now in its adulthood it shimmered ebony black. The ivory-white chin and throat stood out on its black skin. She hardly ever saw Hope, and rarely had to feed the snake. Marie Laveau assumed the snake found lots of food in the cellar of her home. Sometimes she would find its pale yellow molted skin lying on the floor of the basement or on one of the descending steps. Once she got to watch the snake loosen the skin around its mouth and head by rubbing its head against the rough surface of the patio's stone steps. Gradually the snake crawled out of its skin, turning the old skin inside out as it moved.

Marie Laveau looked forward to finding the molted skin at least two or three times a year because then she could make the gris-gris that helped keep her alive. Hope never disappointed her and although free, the snake never abandoned the priestess.

Occasionally Hope would slither into the priestess's bed at night to lie coiled on the extra feather pillow. It allowed the priestess to touch its head, and sometimes stretched out close to Marie Laveau's face, the snake's forked tongue flickering in the air.

Marie Laveau looked out the balcony window at the pounding rain and wondered when it would stop. Usually Hope would visit the priestess at the end of a rainstorm. Hope's scales would be damp, stomach bulging from a recent meal, and it would obviously be seeking a safe place to rest. The next day the priestess would celebrate a ritual in honor of Danbala Wèdo thanking him for sending Hope to bring serenity and peace to her life and also wisdom. The wisdom to mete out revenge before passing on into the spirit world.

Chapter Twenty-two

Sade's mother-in-law spent her time searching for him. She traveled the clubs, the cemeteries, the waterfront, and lastly went to his home though she assumed he would rarely be seeking his own death sleep. She didn't worry about the man who ruined her family's honor. No, she worried about her grandchild, Liliana.

Could someone have the skill to gain power over a vampire's soul? Marie had, and could often feel the soul of the young woman fighting her will. But Marie meant to keep the woman's young, attractive body, and so far had been successful at tamping down the other's soul.

She found Sade one day lurking in a park in the early evening.

"You look awful, Louis." His flesh was almost translucent allowing his veins to cast a blue tinge on his flesh. His normally smooth skin sagged and his face seemed crisscrossed with innumerable lines. His pale blue eyes were silvery and moist.

"What the hell are you doing here?" she asked.

"Waiting for my meal."

"Hell, what will you pick up on this lonely path? A bum?"

"A whore like you, Marie."

"Louis, I'm here to help you, or at least to help Liliana."

"Truth from your lips?" He staggered as if drunk.

"You're spilling too much blood."

"I'm eating for two. Liliana and myself."

"Ridiculous, Louis. Blood can't substitute for the death sleep."

"I will not have that girl manipulated," he roared, striking out with his left hand, causing the nearby tree to lean.

"At least you haven't lost your strength. Your mind maybe."

"Who is doing this, Marie?"

"If I knew I'd bury them in lye."

"Would you even tell me?"

"Louis, you would be freed as a side effect of my protecting Liliana. How do you think that child is bearing up under this? Louis, you must come home with me and I'll . . ."

"Stake me. That would be another way to save Liliana, wouldn't it?"

"No, someone would still have Liliana's soul. The person would be stronger and crueler because they'd also have your soul. We've hated each other, Louis, but I don't hate you anymore. I pity the way you've ruined your life and Liliana's. You've never been a man, Louis. You've remained a boy—a spoiled child who is still searching for his parents' love. They're dead. They're truly resting in peace and don't care the slightest about how you live your life now. Your mother abandoned you for the convent and your father had no time to see to your upbringing. He instead entrusted his most precious possession to his brother, a monk, who didn't know what holy meant."

"Don't preach to me, Marie. I don't want to hear about the past. I don't . . ."

"Think about the past. You do, Louis. Every day you don't sleep the past is coming closer to you. Soon there will be no difference between the death sleep and the past. They'll be so entwined that you'll go mad."

"If you haven't driven me mad, Marie . . ."

"Liliana could drive you mad. The secret you kept from her, the force you used to keep her with you, and the abuse you made her suffer will all come back. You'll live your sins all over again."

"Sins! Marie, do you know me to be a man who worried about sinning?"

"There are special sins you've committed toward Liliana. The ultimate one is that you allowed her destruction."

"I could not save her."

"You should have seen to Liliana instead of that stupid chit that monopolized your time. Why was Liliana at that cemetery? Was she following you?"

"No!"

"How can you be sure? You took away my daughters and Liliana. Thank heaven I prevented you from ruining your sons' lives."

"I didn't particularly like them."

"So it seems one is safest when you don't have a fondness for that person."

"I loved my sons and daughter but you took them away from me. You made them my enemies." He lifted a hand to hit Marie, but she didn't move and Sade lowered his hand without touching her.

"Your wife took her daughter into the convent with her because . . ."

"She was ugly and no man would have her."

"No. She lacked a certain sophistication, but we could have found someone. Never mind. Why are we fighting each other, Louis? We both want to help Liliana's soul, and you certainly have your own to worry about also. This person is gaining more and more strength over you each day because she knows your weak point. Knows of the immense love you had for Liliana."

Sade turned away from Marie, threw his outstretched hands against a boulder, and allowed his muscles to sag.

"Marie, this person had better not be you."

"I'd never use Liliana to get even."

"Your hate for me . . ."

"Please, Louis. You're not all that important to me. Why would I be standing here with you if I were the person responsible?"

"To gawk at what you have done." He turned and faced her again. His eyes were dark with suspicion and rage.

"Fool." Marie spit at the ground before him and walked away.

Chapter Twenty-three

Requiem aeternam dona eis, Domine,
et lux perpetua luceat eis.

Te decet hymnus, Deus in Sion,
et tibi redettur votum in Jersusalem,
exaudi orationem meam,
ad te omnis caro veniet.

Requiem aeternam dona eis, Domine,
et lux perpetua luceat eis.

Kyrie eleison;
Christe eleison;
Kyrie eleison

Marie Laveau's granddaughter sang the last phrasings with the church choir. Sunday she always attended Mass, and this Sunday was a special day. After the main Mass the church choir did a performance of Verdi's *Requiem.*

The local French people filled the church. The doors of the church remained open because so many stood in the doorway.

The granddaughter had arrived early and selected one of the front pews. The choir stood on the altar's steps and the organ player remained tucked away in the loft.

The music filled her with peace. For a while she had forgotten why she had come to Paris. During her time in this church she was a devout Catholic. The gris-gris at her breast was a separate power that also borrowed from her religion. Yes, she was a vodoun priestess, but she also attended confession and made sure she received communion several times a year. In her mind there was no clash of values. She praised the Lord and defended her grandmother.

Her hand shifted from the Bible she held to her chest. The gris-gris rested against her flesh and she knew that wearing it to Mass made the power of the gris-gris stronger. She prayed to the same saints whether celebrating vodoun or attending church services.

Closing her eyes, she visualized her grandmother sitting in the rocking chair by the window. Her grandmother held a set of rosaries in her hands and taught a child kneeling next to her to pray. The granddaughter's lips swept up into a smile seeing herself trying to memorize what prayer went with what bead of the rosary. Sometimes the little girl would lose count of the Hail Marys and her grandmother would remind her to use the beads she grasped in her small hands. And the little girl's rosary was so pretty. A pale pink that glistened in sunlight. The girl loved praying outdoors in the backyard because there she could see God's great work. The trees, the grass, the small animals running up tree barks, and the insects buzzing around her curls. Overhead the blue sky would be smudged with white clouds.

"Excuse me."

The woman next to her had a small child who had become fidgety. The granddaughter opened her eyes and made room for the mother and child to leave.

Marie Laveau's granddaughter made a face at the child, who replied by sticking out his tongue at her. Irked by the intrusion, she began to feel a deep sadness, missing her grandmother and New Orleans.

The choir sang through the *Requiem* without intermission, for which she felt grateful. She hadn't wanted to speak to anyone or to bury her face in her hands as if in prayer.

She didn't depart from the church until most of the congregation had left. The chill in the air made her alert to her surroundings, testing her ability to hold on to the peace she had found inside the church.

She located an available taxi at the end of the block and opened the door. She didn't know Paris well and needed directions.

"I'm interested in locating some of the fancier sex clubs. Would you be able to help me?"

In darkness let me dwell,
the ground shall Sorrow be;
the roof Despair to bar
all cheerful light from me,
the walls of marble black
that moisten'd still shall weep;
my music hellish jarring sounds
to banish friendly sleep.
Thus wedded to my woes
and bedded to my tomb,
O let me living die,
till death do come.

—John Dowland

Chapter Twenty-four

A quarter moon dimly lit the cemetery revealing tombstones, crosses, and mausoleums crowded together. Naked trees sparsely dotted the land. The wind had stripped the trees and blown the leaves onto the graves, where they browned and rotted. The smell of stale, sour flesh surrounded Sade. He could hear the insects chomping on the meat, filling themselves with the putrid feast.

He saw no exit, no gate that would allow him to escape. The cemetery never ended, but he walked. Occasionally he checked a name on a tombstone, cross, or mausoleum. No telling what friends he might encounter while rambling.

A scratching sound attracted his attention. He heard the plop of dirt hitting the ground. Was someone stealing a body? he wondered. There couldn't be a legitimate burial at this hour of the night. He followed the direction of the sound and found a mass of white-and-gray skirt spread across the rear of a woman who dug into the dirt and then threw the earth aside. Coming closer, he noticed that she dug into virgin ground. No marker claimed this earth for the dead.

"Liliana," he whispered, surmising that this had to be a dream.

The woman stopped digging and sat back on her haunches, revealing the face of his dearest niece.

"Again we meet, child. What are you doing?"

"Making a home for myself. It's quiet here and there are many neighbors to keep me company." Her right hand reached out indicating the many markers.

Sade took a few steps, but carefully avoided coming too close to her. He did not want to frighten her away or give indication that he wished to touch the child. He found a clearing and sat.

"This isn't real, Liliana. You can never make a home for your soul and your body doesn't exist anymore."

She looked at her hands. "They dig. See the hole that I've . . ." She turned to indicate where she had been toiling, but the ground was solid; no sign of a grave existed.

"But my hands are dirty," she said, turning back toward Sade.

"Only because you believe them to be dirty. To me they are white and clean. Your nails are perfectly manicured. There are no calluses or breaks in your skin because I see you as perfect."

"You're only talking about how you wish to see me. In reality, if you were honest, you would admit I'm dirty and have broken nails with blood seeping through the flesh where I've worn the skin down."

"No, Liliana, I see perfection and that is my reality because neither of us have substance in this land of dreams."

She wiped her hands on the white-and-gray skirt.

"You see the blood that mars my clothes. You see it, don't you?" Her excited voice saddened Sade.

"No, you are lovely. Nothing stains your skirt, not even the dirt upon which you sit."

She spit upon her palms and rubbed them together.

"No, you're wrong. See, the dirt doesn't even come off with water. I rub my hands and spread the dirt over more flesh." She presented her hands to him. "Don't you see?"

"No, Liliana."

She dropped her hands into her lap and stared at them. "Uncle, where are we?"

"We're dreaming of each other, child. This is not a place. The cemetery is barren, the bodies do not exist, the breeze is a figment, and our bodies are only memories."

She made high-pitched sounds that hurt his ears.

"Uncle, take me home with you. Don't leave me here. Wrap your arms around me and give me time to rest." She spread her arms in invitation.

"I can't do that. You must be strong, Liliana."

"Uncle . . ."

"No! I loved you, Liliana, and I love your memory. But I do not want to see you. You must not give in to your desires. We are forever separate and you must find another way to exist."

"Another way?"

"Do not call to me. Do not allow yourself the pleasure of remembering me. Our love is being used against us."

"Where will I go? From whom can I seek help if not from you?"

"Your peace can only come from you, child. No one can set your soul free if you don't demand it. I don't know your world; therefore I cannot tell you how to accomplish this feat."

"You can try to help. You can try to reach out to me."

"I'm too selfish, Liliana. We would both be dragged down into the depths of despair."

She studied his face for a few seconds. "You don't love me. Grandma was right. You are capable of only loving yourself. You took me because it satisfied your needs. You deserted me when I was no more."

"Liliana, I do love you. But nothing good can come from this crossing of worlds. I still exist in the material world and you do not."

"You're scared of my world, aren't you?" Her features pinched into a glare.

"Not scared. Cautious about entering your world. I know someday I will, but I see no reason to experiment before it is time."

"And will you expect me to guide you when your time has come?"

"No. I know you hate me now. . . ."

"I can't hate you, Uncle. That is why I keep calling to you. When I was small you protected me from Grandma's punishments. When I became an adolescent you shared all your knowledge with me."

"Not all, Liliana. I purposefully omitted telling you of the blood hunger."

"And when I thirsted for blood you taught me how to quench my thirst. You even catered to my dislike for human blood and assisted me in the tasting of animal blood. You brought me gifts of fluffy, petlike animals that I ended up raising because they were too cute to kill. Do you remember? I frustrated you then with my moral restraints, but you didn't turn away from me. You didn't force me to leave your side. You only grumbled and shook your head. I see those times, Uncle. I hear the bark of your anger and the whispers of your consoling voice. I even smell the stench of your body while you slept. You didn't know but I would visit you sometimes. I would sit up close to your coffin, my hands resting on the latch, my cheek pressed against the wood, my nose inhaling your scent from the slight crack between lid and coffin."

"And still you were unhappy, Liliana. You didn't choose to be a vampire and you never would have. I forced the curse on you in a moment of passion and selfishness. I can say I'm sorry, but the words change nothing. I can allow you to wound my soul and still you will be what you are."

"Are you sorry, Uncle?"

"Sorry, yes. But would I do it again?" Sade bowed his head.

"You would." Her soft voice could barely be heard. "Would you have done this to your own daughter?"

Sade sprang to his feet. "It's over, Liliana. Do not punish me for having loved you."

"Shall I hate you for having abandoned me?"

"If you must."

"How can it be so simple for you?"

He turned his back on her to walk away, but felt her hand grip his right ankle.

"Take me with you, Uncle. Please, I beg you. Allow me to stay in your heart."

He heard the rustle of clothes as she dragged herself closer to him to rest her cheek on his leg.

"Don't be pathetic, Liliana. Let me be proud of you."

"Proud? Proud of what? A spirit wandering the earth alone? How can that make you proud?"

Sade looked over his shoulder, reached down with his right hand, and grasped a hank of her hair. He barely hesitated before he pulled her from him and cast her against a nearby tombstone.

"Whoever you are, you will pay for this," he shouted.

Chapter Twenty-five

Exhausted and fevered, Sade pulled himself from his coffin. His hands shook as he lowered the lid back down. He leaned over and heaved several times, leaving spots of blood on the varnished wood. His white hair fell down into his eyes blinding him for a moment to his surroundings.

Swinging his head back and standing tall, he peered around the room. The familiar furnishings, colors, and smells didn't soothe his tortured soul. The room seemed to spin around him forcing him to remember his long life. Dizzy, he stumbled toward the door, reaching out for what appeared to be many doorknobs, each avoiding his grasp.

He closed his eyes to gain control. In the darkness of his mind he found sustaining strength. After several minutes he opened his eyes and focused on the door in front of him. Firmly grasping the doorknob, he opened the door and entered the huge, sparsely furnished living room. Straight ahead beyond the parted drapes he saw the balcony lit brightly by moonshine. Forcing himself to move forward, he opened the glass doors and stepped onto the balcony.

The fresh air cleansed his body of the night's putrefaction. The men and women walking and driving through Paris brought him back to the life he wanted, free of any responsibilities or commitments. Drivers honked and made hand motions at pedestrians. Lovers held hands oblivious of anything outside their union. Dog walkers tugged their charges along hoping to get home to their own suppers. He could see the Eiffel Tower with a bright light at its top warning away planes.

He sniffed the air. His neighbor would have a loin of pork and apples tonight. Smelled almost done, he thought.

Sade unbuttoned his pima cotton shirt allowing his body to feel the soft motion of the breezes.

Tonight he would go out again and wander the clubs seeking respite from the agony. When exhausted, he would return home and be unable to reject the death sleep that sought him at all hours now.

He didn't remember what clubs he had visited the night before, but it didn't matter. All the clubs, all the people blended into a circus menagerie. Some people were clowns, some acrobats that gave him sexual satisfaction. And others angered him or almost made him weep. Names meant nothing. Smiles simply bared teeth and frowns broke the monotony.

He caught the whiff of a mature Rothschild wine being opened. Dinner was served but he wasn't invited. He had to find his own banquet.

Chapter Twenty-six

"Ah, lovely outfit but terribly inappropriate for this club."

The granddaughter faced a man clad in leather from neck to ankles. The suit seemed to glisten as if water had been poured over him, except his hair remained dry and perfectly shaped.

"I come here sometimes, but I'm always disappointed when I see people like you. In London you wouldn't be allowed in a sex club unless you dressed for the scene, but here they let in all sorts."

The man's blue eyes and brown hair matched the paleness of his face. She couldn't know whether the rest of his skin was the same shade and didn't care.

She attempted to go around him, but the crowd prevented her.

"Don't you feel uncomfortable? Bulky turtleneck and baggy trousers doesn't make the scene here. At least take off the sweater. No one will steal it, no one gets cold here." He smirked and revealed typical British teeth—crooked, misshapen.

"I'm looking for someone," she said.

"A husband? A boyfriend? Are you searching out some bad boy? Am I not bad enough for you?"

He turned toward the bar to pick up his drink and as he did, she noticed that his naked rear end protruded out from the leather. After a sip he placed his glass back on the bar and turned to her again.

"May I buy you a drink? Call me Nigel."

She shook her head.

"What would you like? Besides meeting up with your bad boy."

"Monsieur, I'm not here to pick . . ." Her voice faltered. Yes, she did want to pick up a male, but not a mortal one.

He produced two metal pincers that fit in his hand. She didn't know where he had been keeping them except he may have pulled them out of his . . . She didn't want to consider that. He tried to clip the pincers onto her breasts, but she pulled away too quickly.

"Pardon me, *chère*, I didn't mean to almost knock you over."

A man of at least eighty smiled at her. His eager eyes took in her entire body. His bad breath repulsed her.

"If I had known you were looking for old, mademoiselle, I wouldn't have put a rinse in my hair," said the British man.

Her hand went to her right breast and she rubbed her hand gently over the gris-gris.

"I can help you with that itch," the leather-suited man said. "I come here several times a year when I can use business as an excuse. Wife doesn't party much, you see."

"Does she have any idea that you come to the clubs?" she asked.

"No. She wouldn't be interested. 'All this boring sex,' she would say. Never appealed to her. But she's very intelligent and earns almost as much as I do. The children have a nanny, so I couldn't say what kind of mother she would make."

"Why do you stay with her?"

"I told you we have a lot in common, that is, other than sex. No, no, I love my wife, wouldn't think of leaving her."

"I wonder whether she'd say the same if she knew how you spent your time while away from home."

"You're quite morose, not fun at all. Think I'll find myself some better company. Good luck finding a bad boy who'll enjoy being chastised." He laughed. "But I suppose that's what some of these men are looking for. I prefer the reverse."

She watched the man squeeze himself into the crowd. How the hell could she find Sade in this maze of people? She remembered her grandma had told her that *he* would find *her*. The gris-gris would entice him. The same herbs with which she captured him the first time were mixed into the little scarlet bag pinned to her bra. The British man may have been right. She should have taken the time to go home and change before coming here. She didn't have clothes anything like what most of the women wore, but showing a little skin might have assisted the gris-gris.

"He wants blood," a woman said.

"Shhh! Someone will hear you," whispered another female.

"He loves drawing blood. The sex is minor to him. It's the blood."

The granddaughter moved closer to the women who were talking. Dressed in scraps of Lycra and dog collars, the women huddled together near a pillar.

"Everyone agrees it's the blood he seeks. Sometimes I am frightened. I never know how far he will go."

"He whips you that badly?"

"It's not the whipping. He actually takes a bite out of my flesh."

"Cannibal?"

"He doesn't want the flesh. Only the blood."

"If you're so scared, why leave with him at all?"

A long pause followed in which Marie Laveau's granddaughter couldn't be sure whether the women had lowered their voices.

"I don't know. He tells me to follow him and I do. There's a part of me that wants to know how far he will go. My orgasms are always stronger and more frequent with him than with anyone else. And it's because I never know whether I'll survive."

"Is he here tonight?"

"I haven't seen him yet, but it's still early."

"You'll let me know if you see him, won't you?"

"Do you want to leave with us?"

"Maybe."

Marie Laveau's granddaughter decided to keep these young women within sight.

Chapter Twenty-seven

The blood splashed from his back onto the walls. She kept whipping him with hardly a pause between hits. After tying him to the bed, she had gagged him. He couldn't utter the safe word that would make her stop. He couldn't even scream for mercy.

Drenched in blood, the whip carried the crimson liquid into the air. The leather on the whip's handle began to unravel. She didn't feel tired or fearful. What if he died? she had to remind herself. He no doubt had family.

She let go of the whip and it fell onto the peach satin sheets, ruining the color forever.

Marie spread her arms apart, resting her hands on his shoulders, and licked the pools of blood that percolated from the shredded skin. She had tasted sweeter and thicker blood, but the smell drove her mad. He moaned softly, resting briefly, knowing that she hadn't finished.

Marie pulled herself up to sit on his rear. The blood dripped down her chin and spattered her breasts. Her hands fondled her breasts and teased the nipples into hard nubs. She pressed her pubic area into his ass. The slow rocking of her body hypnotized her, carried her forward into sexual freedom. She called out a name but couldn't recognize the sound. Her hands slipped down between her legs and stroked the rising tide flooding her. Her drenched fingers continued to probe and find her sensitive flesh.

She didn't remember the man under her, didn't notice the stickiness of the blood.

"Louis," she groaned.

When she recognized the name, she screamed.

Chapter Twenty-eight

Marie Laveau felt full of anxiety. Her snake Hope hadn't come to her in days, and the tiny snake in the terrarium always watched her.

Her granddaughter hadn't found Sade yet, but he had been where she now stood.

"You are Marie Laveau, child. He will want you for his bed and you will go. You'll lie under him fighting for breath and begging him to stay inside you."

Marie thought back to her first coupling with Sade. She hadn't expected his power to overcome her own. He wove the evening with his words and touches, with his appetite and anger. Yes, she remembered he had been angry. Not at her, but a general anger that she couldn't soothe. She touched his brow and he bit her hand. She wrapped her legs tightly around his waist and he slapped her thighs until they stung. She traced his lips with her tongue and he nibbled on her sensitive skin. She tried to call to him and he stuffed her mouth with his fingers.

Through it all he never slowed his pace, never spoke a tender word. He exchanged his sperm for her blood, and she didn't guess what he was until many months later when he told her.

Out of breath, Marie Laveau rested back into her rocking chair, panting as if she had been with a lover. She rubbed the scarred arm of the rocking chair feeling more of the varnish come off on her hand.

Marie Laveau would bed Sade again. She already awaited him in Paris.

Chapter Twenty-nine

"Still here?" Nigel asked. "Your bad boy hasn't shown up yet?"

Marie Laveau's granddaughter had been bored for over an hour. The young women she had been following about the club hadn't hooked up with anyone, although she gave them credit for trying real hard.

"I'm surprised you're still here," she said.

"Nothing interesting this evening. Mostly tourists like you who freeze up if I say hi."

"Maybe you need to back up into people."

"You noticed. Do you like it?" he asked, turning to give her a special look at his naked derriere. "It can be yours." He wiggled his eyebrows.

"I wouldn't know what to do with it."

"I can give you some ideas." This time he chose to wink.

"I told you I'm looking for a specific someone."

"Have you met him before?"

"No."

"How will you know him? How can you be sure that person isn't me?"

She moved very close to him and he took full advantage by looping his arm around her waist.

"Do you enjoy drinking blood?" she asked.

For a moment Nigel was stunned. "Blood? I am certainly willing to draw blood. But to taste it—I'm afraid that's too dangerous."

The granddaughter said nothing.

"Are you really into drinking blood?"

"No, but I'm looking for someone who is."

"Oh, one of those."

She had been glancing around the club, but when he said "one of those," she turned back to him.

"Is there a special group?"

"Almost half the women have gone off with a guy who frequents this place. And they all talk about his interest in drinking blood. There are a few freaks like that. Think they're vampires. Usually drinkers are young, but there's one middle-aged guy who seems to have captured the interest of many women and a few men."

"Who?" she asked.

"Louis. I had dinner with him one night. By the way, we weren't drinking blood, we had a nice . . ."

"Is he here tonight?"

"What's your name?"

She hesitated, but then made a firm commitment. "Marie Laveau."

"You're not French."

"I'm from New Orleans."

"Yes, your French is a bit strange."

"Nigel, is your friend Louis here tonight?"

"Haven't seen him." He shrugged his shoulders. "I don't think he'd approve of your French."

"That's not what I'm here to offer him."

"Are you sure I wouldn't do? How about if I promise to take a little taste. A pinprick . . ."

"Nigel, get lost."

"What if I see Louis? Shall I steer him away from you?"

"Hopefully I'll see him first."

"Know what he looks like?"

"Would you like me to switch to English so that you can better understand me?"

"He may have seen you first."

Chapter Thirty

Sade noticed Nigel looking back at him. Nigel had been an interesting playmate on several occasions, and now he could help with an introduction to the woman he was speaking to. The woman seemed very familiar. The dark hair that was covered with a black head scarf, called a tignon, the burnt-honey color of the skin, the features fine but also mixed with mulatto, and her build kept throwing him back in time, but he didn't remember the exact decade.

Sade pushed his way through the crowd until he reached Nigel.

"Monsieur, it's been a while since I've seen you," Sade said.

"And it probably would have been a while longer except you managed to spy the pretty lady to whom I'm speaking."

Sade smiled and slapped Nigel's rear end hard. The smack attracted several clubbers including the lady Sade wanted to meet.

"Monsieur," the woman said, extending her hand so that he could kiss her palm.

He took her hand and saw her flinch. Was it the coldness of his touch? He kissed her hand but did not release her.

"Louis, are you going to be stealing another one away from me?"

"It's up to the lady to decide." He looked into her dark eyes and knew her. But, no, that was impossible.

"Nigel, consider yourself a loser." The cruelty in her voice surprised Sade.

"The least I can do is introduce you. Louis, this is Mademoiselle Marie Laveau."

Sade's grip on her hand tightened.

"Ouch!"

"I see you make a perfect couple," said Nigel. "By the way, you'll especially like her. She told me she was into blood games. Sorry I can't join you both but I can see I'm not invited." Nigel slapped Sade on the back before moving away.

"Marie Laveau. That is a familiar name to me, mademoiselle. Although I'm sure there is no connection between you and the woman I knew."

"Why couldn't I be the same woman, monsieur?"

"Because I knew her long ago, long before you were born."

"I am Marie Laveau, the Vodou Queen of New Orleans."

Sade laughed. "You do look very much like her, but I'm sure the one I knew is resting in her grave."

"Because you wouldn't give her eternal life?"

Sade dropped her hand and reevaluated her. Before she

could protest he swept the tignon from her hair. The brown-black curls burst forth from the black material and the long hair settled across her shoulders. He remembered running his fingers through the softness of those curls. He moved toward her and took in the scent of her hair. The same scent that she would leave on the pillowcases. With her hands she reached around his neck and gave him the massage that made those hot nights in New Orleans bearable. He kissed her lips and tasted the spiciness of the foods she used to cook.

"You are far from New Orleans, mademoiselle, yet you bring the flavor of home with you."

"I carry my spices to add to food."

"If you miss the flavors of New Orleans so much, why did you leave?"

"I wanted to find you."

His hands explored her breasts through the black woolen sweater.

"Amazing how well kept you are." He gave her a smile that called her a liar.

"You remember my son Jacques? He died in a shipwreck while crossing the Atlantic. But he adored you."

"Until I bedded his mother."

"He wanted me home with Glapion, true. Yet I don't think he ever hated you. He respected you and fawned on your memory when you left."

Sade nuzzled close to her neck, rolling his tongue over the flesh until he nipped her near her jugular. She almost pulled away and he would have let her go. Instead she stayed in his arms but her breath came in short bursts.

"You are not my Marie Laveau. My Marie Laveau was a brave woman."

"You don't believe. Let's leave here and go someplace where I can reacquaint you with the games we used to play."

Chapter Thirty-one

In New Orleans the weather clung to flesh like a second skin. The streets were quiet and those who moved about chose to take a slow pace. Carriage drivers used buckets of water to wet down their horses. And an old woman sat on her balcony dreaming of another place.

With her eyes shut, Marie Laveau followed the path her granddaughter took, down an alleyway and across a cobbled street to the small apartment she'd taken soon after her arrival. A nearby church guarded the dead in an ancient cemetery. One of the undead walked with his arm wrapped around her granddaughter's shoulders. The old woman's perspiration doubled because of her link with the younger woman.

"Don't be frightened, my sweet. He'll not harm you. It is me that he will eventually seek. By then it will be too late and he will again lose the person most dear to him."

Marie Laveau pressed her hands against the chair's arms and lifted herself to her feet. She wanted no interruption. She turned and limped back into her home closing the glass doors behind her. She pulled the heavy cranberry velvet drapes together, darkening the room. She didn't need to see clearly; she knew her home and knew the path leading to her bedroom. The brightly colored beads interwoven with the iron and brass headboard glittered under the heat and light of the sun. The floral bedspread gleamed in a multicolored patchwork. She had done the crewelwork on the pillows while waiting for her first husband to return. After a year she declared him dead and moved on with her life.

She pulled across the thin linen curtains on the window and practically fell back onto her bed. Up until now she had been sleeping in her rocking chair in the living room. If she lay back, would she be able to lift herself back up? she wondered.

"Sssssss."

Hope had come back after disappearing for over a week. Marie Laveau almost thought she had been deserted. Now Hope came back to lie with her mistress.

"Come, baby," the priestess called. Gently the priestess rested her back against the pile of pillows.

"He's come back, Hope. He doesn't believe it yet but he's come back to me."

Her breath caught as she felt Sade's touch. His hands between her thighs moved her skirt higher. Her hands reached to undo the button on the skirt but, impatient, he tore the material. Her desiccated vagina filled with the moisture of long ago, spilling down her thighs. Her breasts grew plump and soft and ached from desire. Ached for the roughness of his hands and the touch of his tongue upon her nipple. Naked, she invited him into her but he made her wait. Her hand massaged his genitals and she gasped feeling the power she had over him. Taking him into her mouth just the way he had trained her, circling her long tongue around him, pulling back only to touch the tip of his penis with her tongue. And she tasted the saltiness of him and the thickness of his come as drops slipped down her throat.

He grabbed her wrists and forced her back down against the bed and drove into her quickly. Marie Laveau felt Hope skimming up her leg in a slow undulating movement. The scales scratched her old skin but they drove to the same beat. To Sade's rhythm.

Chapter Thirty-two

The cold shower didn't tame Marie's lust. She had actually been fantasizing about having sex with Louis. The cold water kept beating her flesh, punishing her. Her client had left hours ago, a little raw, but his skin would heal. Maintaining control not only of her clients but of her emotions was the important lesson she had learned early in her career as a dominatrix.

After turning off the water, she stood still for a minute before shaking herself like an overgrown terrier.

"Louis," she muttered to herself. "He puts everyone in danger and doesn't care. Even Liliana can't stop that fool. Does he care that the poor child is being used and driven mad by someone who hates him? No, he decides to blame me as if I have no feelings. As if I weren't a woman of sensitivity. I can imagine what is happening to that poor child. Hell, Louis himself sent me to that vacuous world when he destroyed my old body. What a fight I had to come back! Oh, Liliana, if only you were stronger and wiser. You were much too young for the vampire life. Maturity and strength of character are what is needed to become a true vampire."

As she talked to herself, she toweled dry. Dropping the towel, she turned toward her bathroom mirror.

"Louis would be lucky to have you in his bed. He wouldn't be able to keep up with you."

Marie massaged her breasts until her nipples stood at attention. She turned sideways and admired her flat stomach. How come Sade hadn't made a pass at her? she wondered. All this gorgeous flesh tempting him, beckoning each time he saw her.

"Ugh! That's the most disgusting idea I've ever allowed myself. Bedding Louis. Whipping him might not be bad, though." A smile caught up the sides of her lips.

She stood back from the mirror and posed as though she had a whip in her hand and was ready to use it.

Then her thoughts turned to her granddaughter.

This person who controls Liliana's spirit most probably is female and an ex-lover of his. Even considering that most of the women were dead, that would still leave a large mob to choose from.

She and Louis should sit down and make a list of names if he could remember any. Names never meant much to Louis. Maybe they should question every woman in Paris. But she may not be in Paris. His wanderings had taken him to almost every country in the world.

One thing for sure, she couldn't abandon him, because that would mean abandoning Liliana and that she'd never do.

Marie slipped on a sheer silk nightgown.

"It's as if the worms made the material right on my body." She shook her head in wonder and left the bathroom.

In the living room she sat on the white settee that had belonged to Napoleon's Josephine.

"We women have such problems with our men," she commiserated, although she believed Josephine's spirit had moved on to a world she herself would never know.

She hadn't met many of Louis's lovers, always avoided the cheap twits whenever she could. However, Cecelia had certainly been a spiteful bitch. Could she have found a way to make him suffer? Not smart enough. Besides, Cecelia had been way too emotional. Also, the child hadn't looked very well the last time they had been together. Cecelia may be in the same world as Liliana, and Marie imagined that this kind of control had to be practiced by someone living in this world, not wandering that world in a fog.

Marie wondered whether she'd have a better chance if she bedded Louis. That way she could have an idea of what kind of woman might take offense. She sighed.

"There you go again—imagining things so perverse that even you should be ashamed," she yelled at herself. Except that she had no shame. Not the slightest hint of shame. Sure, when human she knew shame, and that jackass son-in-law knew how to stoke it. But after becoming a vampire, shame seemed to vanish. Now she performed acts that she would have had Louis jailed for.

A little bump and grind in the bed with Louis wouldn't be the end of the world. It might mean the end of their peace treaty, though.

Would she herself be jealous over his multitude of partners?

She laughed. Impossible for her to imagine sitting up waiting for the rake. She'd be too busy herself to engage in such a waste of time.

What would her daughters have thought? Especially the older one whom she had guided into marrying Louis.

"I don't think she'd appreciate having her mother bedding her husband. Certainly when her sister went off with Louis she didn't take it calmly."

Of course her children weren't around any more and her own husband had been long dead, so who would care if she slept with Louis?

"I would. I wouldn't be able to live with myself. I'd perform seppuku with a stake."

An ugly sight, she thought. And such a waste of a good body.

Forget the fucking and concentrate on finding the witch who is robbing Liliana of her deserved rest, she reminded herself.

No, she hates me (well-away),
feigning love somewhat to please me,
Knowing if she should display
All her hate, Death soon would seize me,
and of hideous torments ease me.

—Sir Philip Sidney

Chapter Thirty-three

"Uncle, you're back." Liliana ran to Sade and almost hugged him, except that he stepped out of her way.

"Uncle, why do you avoid my touch?"

"Liliana, I'm tired of these dreams."

"Uncle, I don't know what you're talking about."

"Yes, you do. Except you choose to forget our previous meetings."

"Uncle, we're here in . . ."

"Yes, Liliana, where are we? Over here we have a generic tree and over there a gazebo that could be found on any wealthy property. And what are these? Flower beds with perfect lilies and tulips and daisies, and none of these exist at the same time of year."

"This is a backyard." She looked around for a house.

"No, whoever is driving these fantasies didn't bother to build us a home. We don't even need the accessories that we have. All we need to torture ourselves is each other."

"I love you, Uncle. I would never hurt you."

"You do, Liliana. Repeatedly. Every time I'm forced to see you I feel an ache in my gut. Can you believe these brief episodes are enough to bring either of us happiness?"

"Once you loved me. Once you were like a father."

"You have no father, Liliana. Your mother slept with a man and gave birth to you. But that man was no father. I would call him a coward. He didn't want to take you in his arms and love you as a daughter. No, Liliana, he hid. He never once admitted his fatherhood to you. Matter of fact he denied you, tried to say you weren't his. Did you know that?"

"My mother, as you know, died when I was just a toddler. And no one else could be sure of who fathered me."

"Your grandmother knew. And your grandmother wanted it kept a secret. Your father wouldn't dare deny her wish."

"Even *you* fear Grandmother."

"That's right. She had me jailed and put into Charanton, the mental institution. Finally, when I learned how to control my powers I broke free of her. Still, she follows me, making my life hell. I destroyed her body."

"No, Uncle, I don't want to hear this."

Sade moved closer to her but remained out of her reach. "She came back to haunt me and when I cross over to your world I'm sure she'll follow."

"Grandma misunderstands you."

"Wrong. She knows exactly what will disturb me and finds some sort of twisted pleasure in daring me to react."

"I didn't know you destroyed Grandmother." Her eyes welled up with tears.

"Don't cry for that witch. She's back in another woman's body. Another vampire's body, and is thriving."

"She returned to the world?"

"What am I telling you this for?"

"How did she do it, Uncle?"

"I left her skull whole. There is nothing left of you. Look at this. I found your hand and took back my ring. But I saved nothing of yours. Ah, yes, I grieved for a short time."

"For a lifetime or else I wouldn't be here. You want me to be here, Uncle. I feel it."

"You feel whatever spell someone has cast over you, that's all."

"No, it's more than that. You have to want it."

Sade turned away and paced for several minutes.

"Yes, Liliana, I believe you're right. The person who is doing this to us knows the depth of my grief and love."

"Perhaps this person has thrown us together out of pity." She ran to him and grabbed his arm.

"How can you believe that? We may never be together again, Liliana. There is no way for you to come back."

"You're wrong. I can feel how close I am to you. If only you'd help me."

"Never will I love someone the way I loved you. I've banished that kind of love from my heart."

"Please, Uncle, have mercy on me. Don't abandon me to this in-between world. Take me back with you."

"So I can relive the pain?" Sade shook his head.

"The pain is worse now that we are separated." Tears rolled down her cheeks.

"Now you can cry, child. When you were in this world you couldn't. Take comfort in those tears."

"I can't rest. All I can do is cry when you are not with me. Do you think I forget you when you're gone?"

Sade pushed her away. "I forget you."

Chapter Thirty-four

"Louis."

"Marie, how the hell did you get in here?"

"I have my ways. . . ."

"Why?" Sade lay so stunned that he couldn't lift himself out of the coffin.

"I want to help."

"I don't want your help. I've never needed your help. Please go away." He sprang from the coffin, almost knocking Marie over.

"Louis, I know who is bringing these dreams."

"Who?"

"Someone who hates you and knows how much you love Liliana."

"You're telling me nothing new." He thought for a second. "I'm not sure I trust you. I just had a long talk with Liliana about you."

"What did she say? Does she miss me? Does she know about my new body?"

He placed his hands around her neck.

"Not again, Louis. If you destroy me you have no one on your side."

He dropped his hands from her throat and laughed. "You think I'm dependent on you to be on my side? When have you ever been on my side?"

"I've been taking a new look at you. There's really no reason for us to continue to be enemies. We're both vampires and we both engage in sadomasochistic entertainment. Our loved ones are gone so there's no one for me to protect. Besides, I certainly don't look the same."

"Marie, what does your appearance have to do with this?"

"Now, when you first saw my new body and didn't know who I was, you were interested in getting to know me better, right? And now, there's nothing standing in our . . ."

"Oh, Marie, you are not talking about . . ."

"We could gradually work our way into a closer relationship."

"You're far too close right now. Marie, I will never bed you. I don't want to lay a finger on you."

"Ah, the dance continues . . . kinda teasing each other until we'll no longer be able to stand it. When you think about it, Louis, that's what we've been doing all along."

"Get out!"

"Louis, you need some time to digest this. You can be quite slow at catching on to certain kinds of emotion. When you fully gain insight into this . . ."

"Marie, I already have enough people playing with my soul."

"Liliana and the person controlling the both of you?"

"Three if you figure the person I slept with last night."

"Oh. Is this a woman you've just met?"

"Don't do this, Marie."

"Why can't I ask? I've finally arrived at this understanding, this huge insight into why we can't get along, and now you want to leave me."

Sade turned to leave the room.

"Calm down. We should make a list of women who would do this to you. It has the woman's touch. Men just go for brutality, but a woman would wisely choose love as a weapon."

Chapter Thirty-five

Marie Laveau's granddaughter knelt at the communion rail in the small church just up the street from where she stayed. The first contact with the cold marble had made her shiver, but soon the pain in her knees made her sweat.

"Dear Lord, forgive me. I must avenge my grandmother. I do not do these things to hurt You and will find a way to make it up to You." She held the rosary her grandmother had given her.

"From her I learned how to contact the good spirits and saints. Now we both play with the lost souls, the undead. They are under our control now and we intend to end the cruelties. They have pummeled your innocent souls for their pleasure, taking their right to praise You. Instead the innocent must hide from You and know You will finally reject them. Grandmother and I will save the ones who haven't been spoiled. Grandmother calls it revenge, but I know I'm also saving Your precious souls."

The young woman looked down at her wrists and saw the

black and blue marks and wondered whether in the process of seeking revenge she would be abandoned by God.

The organ started up. Choir practice, she thought, but when she turned and peered up at the choir loft, no one was there. The organ sat empty. Her hand sought the gris-gris her grandmother had given to her. Can it be that her grandmother calls to her? she wondered.

"Lord, forgive my grandmother. She has been a good woman in many ways. She cared for those who suffered yellow fever. She visited the condemned in the Louisiana jails to bring some last comfort to men who had lost their way. She has always used her gifts to help or protect. Never has she done anything spiteful except for this one time. But he is not one of Yours. He follows the devil and will continue to bring others to Your foe."

Her eyes scanned the church, seeing the old statues, the stained-glass windows, and line after line of pews.

She recalled her mother taking her as a little girl to church every Sunday and on holidays. Before she made her first Holy Communion she would wait impatiently for her mother to return to the pew. Carrying the Lord inside her, her mother would kneel and ignore the child until she had given her thanks to God. The child waited in awe for her mother to finish her private talk with God, and wanted to know what they said to each other. She thought she would know when it was her turn to receive Christ's body and blood. But she had never heard His voice, never felt His hand rest on her shoulder, and never felt His strength make her toil easier.

"Are You there, Lord?"

Chapter Thirty-six

"Now this woman you've met," Marie continued.

"Can't you leave me alone?"

"If I do that, where does that put Liliana? Waiting on you to figure out the bitch who is doing this?"

"It's partly Liliana's fault."

"Her fault?" Marie crossed the room to sit down on the couch next to Sade.

"If she were stronger she could fight off this cursed witch or whatever."

"And what about you?"

"I'm at fault too. I met a woman the other day who calls herself Marie Laveau."

"That vodou queen down in New Orleans? She must be very old."

"Young. Too young to be Marie Laveau. Too young to even be an experienced vodou queen."

"What's the matter with you, Louis? She has to be practicing some sort of mojo over you."

"Too young to have enough power to take on spirits and vampires. Nineteen, twenty."

"Seems to me she's had plenty of time to learn the trade. Why are you refusing to consider her?"

"I'm not refusing. I'm . . . uncomfortable with the idea that she may really be Marie Laveau. We had sex and she performed the routine like we had just been to bed the night before."

"Does she claim to be the original Marie Laveau?"

"Yes, but something isn't right. Marie Laveau had spirit. She could be tender and caring and cruel. This Marie Laveau isn't sure of herself. I frighten her."

"So maybe you should go easy in the whippings."

"No, Marie, I didn't whip her."

"Sounds rather boring. . . ."

"No, the opposite. As I said before, she knows how to play my body and how to respond to my needs."

"Oh, she's too perfect."

"Exactly! She has every move memorized. It isn't spontaneous." Sade paced the living room.

"You mean she has learned how to respond to you instead of her actions coming from her gut."

"I believe Marie Laveau is alive but she's not the woman I had sex with last night."

"Of course not, she'd be a corpse if she were the real Marie Laveau, like us."

"Not like us. Marie Laveau asked me to make her a vampire and I refused."

"Why?"

"I didn't want the damn woman following me around for centuries, like you do."

"Louis, we are bound together. You need me . . . in a sense."

"Not by choice."

"Think of me as the bastard child. The one you'd rather keep in the closet but I'm still part of you. Your blood made me a vampire."

"When will you ever let me forget?"

"Never. Marie Laveau was very powerful, am I right?"

"Yes, Marie."

"And you rejected her?"

"You're going to tell me that she's the one entering my sleep."

"Why not?"

"She wasn't vicious, unlike you."

"She's had a long time to stew over your rejection. And by now her age would make her life difficult. The pains, the aches, the glances in the mirror."

"We parted on good terms."

"You said 'good-bye' and she managed to keep her tears under control until you walked out the door. Is that what you mean?"

"Damn!" Sade hit the living room wall with his right fist. The plaster shattered, spraying his clothes with white powder. "That girl better not be the person responsible for what's happening to Liliana and me."

"Louis, you give me chills when you rage." She smiled wantonly.

Chapter Thirty-seven

The granddaughter ran the bath and lightly sprinkled sudsing bubbles into the water. She laid towels on the bathroom bars to heat. The mirror already had started to fog over. She slipped the robe from her shoulders and stepped into the fragrant water. She settled down and noticed that the water almost overflowed the tub. She shut the faucets off and leaned back against the porcelain tub.

Last night she had performed perfectly with the help of her grandmother. She had given Sade and her grandmother free rein over her body. Her own flesh numbed at Sade's touch, but her grandmother had felt every stroke and kiss, responding as if she were in his arms.

But the granddaughter felt unclean. Her flesh showed the bruises, bites, and the sticky crust of his sperm. She used her hands to rub her thighs, causing them to flush a bright red. Her eyes watered and she shut them while stretching her tired body.

"Grandmother, how long must I succumb to this man's lust?"

Many times the young woman had been possessed by spirits during vodoun rituals. Never did she remember what she had done during the dances; instead she woke exhausted, disoriented. But last night she knew everything that had happened. Grandmother hadn't allowed the woman to escape into a total limbo; instead she'd forced her granddaughter to watch. Forced the granddaughter to see the pleasure he took from her body and watch his attempt to draw her into the play.

He never suspected that she had felt nothing. Never knew that it was the real Marie Laveau who responded with her orgasms. The old woman in New Orleans writhed and panted through her granddaughter. The young Marie Laveau watched the pornographic images and wished she could partake. But that could never be for as long as her grandmother required control. The young Marie Laveau would have the scars but none of the pleasures.

Why did Sade hate the dreams sent to him by her grandmother? He got to be with a woman he loved, even feeling her flesh, deriving pleasure from the apparent proximity. Far worse to watch and not be able to partake.

She splashed the water with her legs and spattered the tiles with soap suds. Stopping, she realized her sullen snit would not change the situation the way it had when she was a little girl.

Grandmother had bought her anything she had wanted. Double scoops of ice cream, cotton candy, pralines dipped in chocolate, beignets sprinkled with powdered sugar, and jambalaya filled with sausage and fish.

The young woman giggled thinking how strange that

all her favorite moments involved food. Yet the only other times she recalled with her grandmother involved the frightening vodoun lessons. Many times they engaged in strange chemistry experiments with substances both beautiful and foul. Frogs' legs with the blood still dripping from them could be thrown into a heavy cast-iron pot with a person's fingernails or bits of hair from either the skull or the pubic area depending on the spell. Birds' eggs with tiny embryos floating around in the yolk always made her stomach tighten.

Grandmother told her to be a brave little girl. Told her to keep still when she wanted to scream. Taught her to hold and touch things that made her nauseous. Required the little girl to dig in dirt to find insects needed to complete the potions.

She looked at her long manicured nails, now so pristine and brightly colored.

"I love you, Grandmother."

And what else? What did she suppress? What couldn't she admit to her grandmother?

"I love you, Grandmother," she repeated. "Always will love you. No one can ever be as important to me."

As important and what else?

She blanked on the words. Didn't want Grandmother to hear. Grandmother with the wrinkled skin, shiny eyes, missing teeth, and tremors.

Grandmother had never spanked the way her own mother had. Grandmother never raised her voice. Never gave the wicked eye when angry. Yet she . . .

"No. I love Grandmother and that is why I obey."

Chapter Thirty-eight

Sade ground his teeth thinking about the beautiful Marie Laveau, so like the woman he had slept with the other night, and yet he knew she couldn't be alive. Unless her vodou skills had truly grown over the years. Grown to the point that she controlled the aging process.

He had meant to have sex only once with the mysterious young woman calling herself Marie Laveau, but no one else seemed as fetching to him. Fetching, no. Sex-starved. The woman had been making up for a long period of chastity. Strange considering her beauty.

He had walked by her apartment several times that evening, but never dared to stop. He hated to believe that she might be the cause of Liliana's pain and his own suffering. His mother-in-law certainly believed Marie Laveau had something to do with his dreams. How often had the Vodou Queen told him how she controlled the spirits? He had laughed at her sincerity thinking she only imagined the control she professed.

"Monsieur, do you have a light?" asked a woman in a micro-mini.

"Mademoiselle, you'll catch a cold dressed the way you are."

The woman smiled and used her hand to raise the skirt higher until he could view the thong underwear that hugged her hips.

"Would you like to take me in for the night, monsieur? Prevent my coming down with pleurisy?"

"You could come down with far worse going home with strangers, mademoiselle."

She grinned, reached into her purse, and pulled out condoms.

"And how much do those condoms cost?"

"The way you're dressed, monsieur, I'm sure you can afford them."

Quickly Sade reached out and grabbed her arm to pull her close.

"Ouch! Your grip is too tight, monsieur."

"Ah, you are too delicate to be entertaining."

"You would beat me instead of your wife, monsieur?"

"No, I would beat both of you." He looked up at the window to Marie Laveau's apartment. He wondered whether she would welcome him with this stranger. "You are right, I can easily afford your time."

"Enough to cover any doctor bills, monsieur?"

"I will pay you extra if you believe a doctor is needed."

"There'll be another woman?"

"Only one."

"And where will we go?"

"Two doors down and three flights up."

Chapter Thirty-nine

The granddaughter rubbed lotion over her body, enjoying the feel of her fingers against her flesh. She had wiped the mirror clear and stared at her face. Her face or her grandmother's face? The shape and color of their eyes matched. Her brows had been thinned by her grandmother to imitate a certain time in her life. Both had honey-sweet complexions and slightly oversized nostrils. Their lips differed. The granddaughter had chapped and split lips from the bruising way Sade had made love. She imagined her grandmother with smooth, red-tinted lips that were brushed with kisses only when the granddaughter visited.

Her hand touched the mirror outlining the reflection of her lips. Deceptively smooth in the reflection, she thought.

A bundle of tight, wet curls circled her face. The curls would soften when her hair dried and the color would slightly lighten.

Naked, she walked out of the bathroom into the hall

enjoying the cool air on her body. The bruises had yellowed and her skin felt squeaky clean.

While near the front door, she heard the elevator doors open and heard voices mixed with giggling. She touched the door and called upon her senses.

"What do you think she'll say when she sees me, monsieur? Is your wife very jealous? I get paid even if she throws me out, right?"

Finally the male voice answered. "If you wish I will give you the money now."

The granddaughter recognized Sade's voice.

"I charge according to the amount of time and the kinds of things you request."

Silence.

"Ah, I'd stay a month for this kind of money, monsieur."

Before Sade could knock, the granddaughter opened the door.

"Perhaps I'm not really such a surprise, monsieur," said the prostitute.

"Marie Laveau, I'd like you to meet . . ." Sade waited patiently while the prostitute took in the situation.

"Nannette," she said.

The granddaughter didn't have to bother to invite them in because Sade entered her home as if it were his own. The prostitute followed.

"I guess we'll get right down to business," said Nannette, removing her clothes as she checked out the interior of the apartment. "Wouldn't happen to have champagne?"

Silently the granddaughter walked to the kitchen. When she opened the refrigerator door Sade's cold hands slid down her derriere. He leaned in to whisper in her ear.

"Did you sense my arrival?" he asked.

"I expected you all evening," she said, turning and handing him a fresh bottle of champagne.

He took the bottle and read the label.

"Nannette is merely a prostitute, my dear. This brand should be kept for more deserving company."

"Ah, but you'll want some. Besides, that's all I've got."

"Nannette," he called.

The naked prostitute entered the kitchen.

"Will this do, Nannette?" he asked.

"Only one bottle?" Nannette seemed disappointed and in need of something to steady her nerves. "As I recall, it is always recommended that the host should allow one bottle per person."

The granddaughter reached into the refrigerator and pulled out another bottle.

"This is for you, Nannette. Sade and I will share the other bottle."

Nannette grabbed the bottle offered by the granddaughter.

"Please yourselves." She started to walk out of the kitchen when she remembered something. "A light. I still need a light, monsieur."

Nannette had never laid down her cigarette.

Chapter Forty

A group of tourists followed a black-suited man in tails with a black cape lined in blood red. The greased black hair on the guide's head supposedly made him look like Bela Lugosi. However, his Southern drawl ruined the effect. His black fingernails helped point out the important attractions. Bloodthirsty murders took place in almost every other house and ghosts moaned and groaned most of the night except when tourists happened by.

Marie Laveau waved down at the guide and he saluted her with a bow. The gawkers became transfixed by the ancient soul on the balcony. A witch, around for centuries, the guide warned them. Stay clear of her for she is very powerful. Before moving on, the guide winked up at Marie.

He didn't believe in the power of vodou, but she liked him anyway. His father had been one of her students, but the boy had been allowed to stray from the religion.

"Atheist," she mumbled. And gave a weak wave at the guide's back.

She moved back inside her apartment. Her heart leapt when Hope startled her with a strange hissing sound. The snake waved the raised upper portion of its body in a hypnotic sway.

"What's wrong, Hope? You have had too much to eat?"

The snake darted at Marie Laveau but never touched her.

A warm flush rapidly moved through Marie Laveau's body.

"He's back, Hope. That's what you sense, isn't it?"

His hands and mouth explored while she reached for him, but he grabbed her wrists, forcing her back. She heard the glass door to the patio shake. The smooth, clear glass lowered the fever in her old body allowing her to breathe again. She felt his tongue follow the convolutions of her right ear, making her body shiver.

Hope slithered along Marie Laveau's dress until its own tongue touched her mistress's tongue. The snake's forked tongue played against the roof of Marie Laveau's mouth increasing the rising lust. Marie Laveau touched the snake's body feeling the bulge of that evening's dinner. The snake's scales abraded Marie Laveau's fingertips and she felt tiny thin trickles of blood spill onto the snake. Hope's body went into spasms and the bulge moved farther down its body.

Marie Laveau felt the weight of Sade slip between her thighs and push into her body. Her hips pressed outward wanting him deeper inside her. The snake clung to her body as her hands pressed against the scales now causing many of the scales to fall off.

"Yes," she whispered. Then all stopped. There were other hands. Hands pulling him away from her. Hands roughly abusing her breasts. Dirty hands. Hands that fumbled in a drunken stupor.

Another woman set her mouth to his balls and struggled to tempt him out of Marie Laveau. Hope hissed close to her mistress's ear.

Sade had included an outsider in the ménage à trois.

Marie Laveau sensed the body odor of a mortal. A powerless mortal, she decided. She raised her bloodied fingers to her mouth and sucked.

"Blood, my love. Warm blood to keep us both alive. Taste my tongue. Recognize the demand of your body, my love. Her flesh is warm with the flowing blood."

Marie Laveau took her fingers from her mouth and transferred the blood onto Hope's tongue.

"Sweet, isn't it?"

Hope's tongue flicked out into the air sending the stench and taste off to her mistress's lover. He exploded inside her, but in a rush she felt his weight ease off her body.

"Yes, drink up." She swallowed, imagining the blood running down her own throat. "Take it all. Don't leave her alive. Gift me with her soul."

The snake slithered away from her mistress, hiding from the coming death, making room for the new soul.

Marie Laveau reached out and grabbed at a breeze that wandered through the window. The air fidgeted within her clasped hands and she brought her fists to her mouth and swallowed Nannette's soul.

Chapter Forty-one

With her body rolled into a ball, the granddaughter stared at the vision before her. Blood covered the sheets. Nannette lay lifeless under Sade's bite. The granddaughter had watched his throat as he drank from the prostitute. The movement of his Adam's apple rapid, animalistic. Her hands traveled down between her thighs and felt his sperm dripping from her. She wanted to flush her vagina but, afraid to move, she waited.

Sade sank heavily onto Nannette's body. He appeared as lifeless as his victim.

The granddaughter wondered whether she could move. Would he notice if she fled? Could she move slowly and not disturb his rest? Would he fall asleep here in her bed and dream? This frightened her. She didn't want to be near him when her grandmother's magic took hold.

Sade rolled over onto his back, thrusting his arms out across the bed. Blood stained his chin and chest. No longer wet, the blood took on a different color. Darker.

Sade turned, raising himself up on his elbows, and glared at her.

"This is your doing, bitch. You brought this hunger on."

She shook her head, didn't have an answer for him.

"Why? Tell me why you would want this." His head motioned toward the dead body.

Again her head shook and her body pressed against the burl headboard.

She didn't see him move, but suddenly he gripped both her arms.

"You have a power over me, don't you?"

She swallowed, trying to clear her throat for words. Her knees pressed against his chest.

"Damn you, speak to me. Tell me what you want!" His voice caused a ringing inside her ears.

Her lips moved but she had forgotten how to speak.

He shook her. "Do you know about Liliana?"

Her muscles began to cramp. The pain caused her eyes to water.

"You know who I am. Who told you? You can't be the Marie Laveau I knew. A daughter. No, a granddaughter. That's why you look so like her. You're playing at games that should have died with your grandmother."

He threw her backward, her own head hitting the bed's wooden headboard. He began ripping the sheets off the bed, emptying the pillowcases. She saw how he easily flung the body from the bed. Raving, he stormed the apartment searching for something.

Finally he came back to the bedroom.

"What a fool I am," he said.

Rushing toward her, he lifted her into the air, tossing her down on top of the dead body that had started to cool. He flipped the mattress and saw the scarlet threads. He lifted the small satchel and gripped it tight in his hands.

"Gris-gris! What's this for? Is this what ties Liliana and me to you? Just a few grains of dirt?"

She rolled off the dead body and was able to get to her knees. She tried reaching out for the red satchel, but he kept it away from her.

"You want it back. Why would I give it back to you?"

"It doesn't bind you to me," she whispered. "It's meant for my own protection. She gave it to me so that I would be sure to return home."

Sade's brow arched. "Who gave this to you? Who?"

Startled by his yell, she stuttered before replying. "My grandmother."

"Marie Laveau?"

"There have been Marie Laveaus for many generations."

He hovered over her. "But the one that made this gris-gris is the one that I knew, isn't she?"

"I'm too young to . . ."

"Don't try to play with words. I bedded this woman and left her to return to her family. Her weak-willed husband. She wanted everlasting life and I refused to give it to her. But she's used her spells and hexes to keep herself alive, hasn't she?"

He rushed across the room and opened the double windows. He unfastened the tie on the scarlet bag and emptied the contents into his hand.

"No, please. Give it back to me. It cannot harm you," she pleaded.

"But you can," he said, releasing the contents into the night breeze.

Chapter Forty-two

An icy stillness filled Marie Laveau's living room. Her body felt relieved of a burden, but also lost. She reached out with her mind and searched for her granddaughter. A void lay to all sides of her. Emptiness, fear, and loss filled her soul. The threads binding her to her granddaughter had been broken.

What had her granddaughter done? Had she lost the gris-gris? Had Sade found the gris-gris? He certainly would waste no time in destroying the small satchel.

Marie Laveau sat in her chair and turned to the terrarium on the table next to her. The pygmy rattlesnake lay as still as always and seemed to be watching her, waiting for her to make a wrong move, waiting to be freed. She fed the rattlesnake regularly but it always appeared to be hungry. Not for food but for revenge. It slithered up against the glass nearest its mistress and pressed against the glass inviting a touch, inviting a foolish move.

"No, dear one, I have a purpose for you but it is not time to set you free." She ran her right index finger against the glass and watched as the snake struck out. "Mamma is only teasing. I shouldn't enrage you, but I want you keep your anger fresh. Don't let it pass into limpid acceptance. Soon we may have a visitor. One that I've been waiting a century for. He'll find me. And I'll be here as I always am. Waiting. Expecting."

Marie Laveau dropped her hands back into her lap. The rattlesnake slowly slipped from the glass, disappointed and sullen.

"Sorry, babies." She apologized to the rattlesnake and her granddaughter. She had been forced to use the most precious lives in the world.

She rocked in her chair wondering whether Sade's blood hunger could have driven him to kill her own granddaughter. Marie Laveau had only wanted the soul of the stranger in order to bind Sade closer to her. She hadn't thought beyond the power she would gain. She hadn't considered her granddaughter's safety, assuming the bag of gris-gris would perform its work. She had no phone, no modern way of reaching her granddaughter. Usually, even without the gris-gris, she had always been able to at least sense the presence of her granddaughter in the world. Nothing now sang to her of her precious child.

She closed her eyes and found the brute force Sade emitted. His anger flared hot, but everything else around him remained frozen. He would soon need to rest.

Marie Laveau flicked a finger beckoning a soul forth, demanding that it come before her to do her bidding.

Confusion, pain entered Marie Laveau's mind and she knew that Liliana had come.

What is my hand doing?
It caresses: soft, soft, soft
It pinches: ouch, ouch, ouch
It tickles: tickle, tickle, tickle
It scratches: scratch, scratch, scratch
It hits: whack, whack, whack
It dances: twirl, twirl, twirl
And then . . . it goes away!

—French Nursery Rhyme

Join the Leisure Horror Book Club and

GET 2 FREE BOOKS NOW—

An $11.98 value!

Yes! I want to subscribe to the Leisure Horror Book Club.

Please send me my **2 FREE BOOKS**. I have enclosed $2.00 for shipping/handling. Each month I'll receive the two newest Leisure Horror selections to preview for 10 days. If I decide to keep them, I will pay the Special Members Only discounted price of just $4.25 each, a total of $8.50, plus $2.00 shipping/handling. This is a **SAVINGS OF AT LEAST $3.48** off the bookstore price. There is no minimum number of books I must buy and I may cancel the program at any time. In any case, the **2 FREE BOOKS** are mine to keep.

Not available in Canada.

NAME: ______________________________

ADDRESS: ______________________________

CITY: ____________________ **STATE:** __________

COUNTRY: ____________________ **ZIP:** __________

TELEPHONE: ______________________________

E-MAIL: ______________________________

SIGNATURE: ______________________________

If under 18, Parent or Guardian must sign. Terms, prices, and conditions subject to change. Subscription subject to acceptance. Dorchester Publishing reserves the right to reject any order or cancel any subscription.

The Best in Horror!
Get Two Books Totally FREE!

An $11.98 Value! FREE!

PLEASE RUSH MY TWO FREE BOOKS TO ME RIGHT AWAY!

Enclose this card with $2.00
in an envelope and send to:

Leisure Horror Book Club
20 Academy Street
Norwalk, CT 06850-4032

Chapter Forty-three

Sade found himself in a maze. The tall hedges blocked his view and the thick vines prevented him from breaking through. The sandy path turned to the right and left in front of him and when he turned there was only a wall of hedges.

Nothing to do but move forward, he thought, realizing instantly that he must be in a dream and soon he would find Liliana.

His body sweated as his flesh had done when mortal. His silk shirt clung to his body and his jeans rubbed roughly against his thighs. He opened the shirt and thought about taking it off, but wondered whether that slight change would make him more vulnerable. He certainly felt desperate if he thought a mere shirt could be his armor. He laughed at the idea, but kept his shirt on.

"Liliana," he called, wanting this to be over. "Liliana, I'm here. I think I know who is behind this dreaming business."

The hedges shimmered, almost fading.

"Come now, Marie Laveau, you must have known I eventually would recognize your work. What did you send to me? A child of your flesh? Or a zombi masked to look exactly like you?"

"Uncle."

He recognized Liliana's panicked voice, stabbing him in the heart.

"Here, Liliana. We cannot be far from each other. What do you see?"

"Hedges. I'm surrounded by hedges. I keep trying to break off the vines and they quickly grow back. They grow back faster than I can remove them."

Sade reached the fork of the path.

"Keep talking, Liliana."

"I'm frightened. What if I am never able to escape?"

Her voice echoed all around him. Going left, going right didn't seem to make a difference because her voice told him she awaited him no matter what turn he took. He cut to the right and saw a fountain. A huge stone head bubbled water from its mouth. He backtracked and took the left turn, only to find the same fountain.

"Ouch!"

"Liliana, what happened?"

"The hedges are growing thorns. Large thorns that prevent me from reaching through them."

"Liliana, stop trying to free yourself. Wait for me to find you."

"You'll never find me."

"Liliana, remember how you danced for me. I can still see the little girl twirling around in circles, laughing and making herself dizzy. Do you remember the dance?"

"Uncle, I cannot . . ."

"Yes, you can, Liliana. Close your eyes and see yourself as a child. You wore the gaudy multicolored dress that you prized."

"Silly. I looked like a Gypsy child in it."

"But in it you always shined brightly."

"Grandmother made fun of me. Perhaps that's why I wore the silly dress so often."

"I hope so."

"I loved the soft material and refused to wear underclothes because I wanted the fabric close against me. Sometimes I even slept in the dress. When Grandmother came in to say good night, I would pull the covers up to my chin and hold my breath hoping she wouldn't catch me in the dress. She never did, although she did think me odd at times." Liliana giggled with the memory.

Even Sade smiled in recognition of the memory.

"Ow!"

"What is it, Liliana?"

"The dress I'm wearing has turned into thistles. They scratch my skin and leave marks."

"You've opened your eyes, Liliana. Close them again and remember my fingers tickling your body. You would giggle so hard that the giggles would turn into hiccups."

"Sometimes you would tickle me before bed and Grandmother would yell at you, but that only made the situation funnier and I would continue to laugh. And then she would become impatient and hit me. She would smack my behind but never hard. I knew she did it only for show and to make you feel bad."

"And then she and I would argue as always."

"I always rooted for you, Uncle. Even when Grandma

and Grandpa told me that you did bad things. I couldn't imagine what bad things you could be doing and my grandparents never detailed your exploits."

"Just as well, Liliana. My travels, my books, the company I kept didn't deserve presentation to such a young innocent child."

Again the hedges shimmered. He knew Marie Laveau must be angry because he so adeptly calmed his niece. She wants us both to cry, he reminded himself. She wants us to weep over our separation when instead we have so much to recall.

"Uncle?"

"Yes, Liliana."

"Must I keep my eyes closed forever? Will the current world never be as beautiful as the past?"

He didn't know how to answer the question. He didn't want to steal away her hope. But he didn't want to lie.

"If something is beautiful and amusing to remember, why leave the memory, Liliana?"

"Because I want to make new memories, Uncle."

"I will come for you, Marie Laveau, and whatever you have planned I will not fear." Sade muttered these words quietly, hoping his niece would not hear.

"Who is Marie Laveau, Uncle? Is she a woman you've bedded?"

"She is a woman who has cruelly abused us."

Chapter Forty-four

Sade awoke with a calmness he hadn't felt in a long time. When he pushed up the lid of his coffin, the sun caught him within its full force. He hadn't remembered to close the drapes and he hadn't slept the day away. At first the sunlight blinded him, but he managed to swing himself out of the coffin. He didn't bother to close the drapes; instead he headed for the bedroom door and entered the dim hallway.

His flesh felt tight under his clothes. He hadn't bathed the night before, and the blood of his latest victim still clung fast to his flesh.

He had thought about taking the imposter's blood, but didn't know whether it would be safe. Had the Marie Laveau he bedded been a real mortal, or could the flesh have been raised from a grave and animated only to entice him? Drinking the stale blood of a zombi would probably only cause sickness and then hunger after he had spit the foul brew of blood up.

He had left the young woman alone. He hadn't bothered to destroy her because he didn't know what kind of curse could have been attached to that. He had left her with the dead prostitute. He wondered whether she would make it back to New Orleans and the real Marie Laveau before he did. It didn't matter because Marie Laveau already knew he was on to her.

He spent over an hour in the bathroom letting the warm water cleanse his stale-smelling flesh. He lost all sense of time with his plotting and planning. He hadn't been to the States in a while, and hadn't wanted to return just now, but necessity took away his own personal choice. Finally he threw on a silk robe.

When he entered the living room he noticed that the sunset had begun. Shadows spread across the room hiding traces of dust and darkening the wooden furniture.

The doorbell rang and Sade answered.

"Just the person I wanted to see, my mother-in-law." Sade left the front door open, but immediately returned to the living room.

"Louis, I wish you would stop calling me your mother-in-law. My daughter has been dead for centuries. By now we should be on friendlier terms."

"Bedmates?" he asked.

"It may take a while, but why not?"

Sade grunted and flung himself into the nearest leather chair.

"You're in a foul mood. Have you been dreaming again, Louis?" She planted herself on the arm of Sade's chair.

"Whenever I seek my death sleep I dream now. You know that."

"Still don't know who is causing the dreams?"

Sade stood and headed to his bedroom to get dressed.

"You do suspect some—"

The bedroom door slammed in her face and she heard the lock catch.

"I'm here to help you, Louis. Why don't you let me? Besides you must admit that we both have an interest in Liliana's peace."

She heard glass breaking, and hoped it wasn't the expensive vase she hoped to inherit.

"Louis, we must . . ."

The door opened and a leather-clad Sade pushed past Marie.

"Where are you going?"

"Taking the motorcycle out. Want to join me?"

"I work hard keeping this body beautiful. Do you think I want to go on one of your maniac rides and ruin all the work I've done?"

"Be daring," he gibed.

"Louis, riding around with the wind in your hair isn't going to solve this problem."

"I'm running errands, Marie, not just passing time."

"You're going after the person responsible for your dreams, aren't you?"

"Yes," he said, digging keys out of his jacket.

"And who is this person?"

"The woman is after me, not you."

"Who is she? You must let me help. I'm a woman and can give you some idea of how women think."

"No woman thinks like you, Marie."

"This one does. She obviously wants to destroy you. And for a while I shared that goal."

"Now you're in love with me," he said, looking at her with a wry smile.

"Lust is the word. I lust for you. Quite a bit different than love."

"I believe this woman loved me at one time, and you can't say that."

"Did she ever love you, Louis? Or did she abuse you in the same way you abused her? Plus you have a gift that many would wish for."

"Being made a vampire." Sade stood still, remembering the Vodou Queen pleading with him for eternal life. "She did want the 'gift' as you call it. Marie Laveau . . ."

"Ah, the Vodou Queen. No wonder she can reach Liliana."

"Marie Laveau remained patient all through our relationship. I knew what she wanted. She had made it clear early on, but she never nagged, never threatened. She probably believed I would take her with me when I decided to move on."

"Sounds as if she was in love."

"No, patient."

He watched Marie pull back from him. Her eyes steady on his, her face a mask.

"What's wrong?" he asked.

"What if she had been in love with you? If you had been sure of her love, would you have given her the gift?"

"Dammit, Marie, stop calling being a vampire a 'gift.' I never asked to be a vampire. I never considered it a gift."

"You've never told me who changed you." Marie's voice seemed unusually soft.

Sade gripped the keys tightly in his hands, feeling the

sharp teeth cut into his flesh. Marie moved closer and touched his arm.

"You're going to New Orleans. Let me come with you for support. You'll need to feel that someone is on your side when you face that woman's evil spirits."

"You, on my side? I'd like to lock up now." Sade walked to the front door, pulled it open, and waited for Marie to exit. She started to leave but stopped.

"You know I'll go to New Orleans anyway. Wouldn't it be better to be aware of what my plans are?"

"You'd never tell me the truth."

Marie nodded and left.

Chapter Forty-five

Lost on the dark streets, the granddaughter sought a hallway or alcove in which she could rest. Returning to her room would be impossible. She had left in a hurry immediately after Sade had abandoned her as he had abandoned her grandmother centuries ago. He had dispatched her gris-gris in the breeze, dressed, stepped over the dead, and left. The whole time she had stayed out of his way, frightened by his anger and confused.

Far away in New Orleans she had been confident in her ability to control the vampire. She had thought her grandmother foolish to worry, and now she hid in the dark shadows of Paris. Afraid of everyone. Terrorized by the vampire she had sworn to make suffer.

No doubt the dead woman on the floor of her apartment had been a prostitute. Perhaps not an individual who would cause a major search, but eventually the smell would draw attention and she wanted to be out of Paris by then. How could she explain the scene in her room?

The police certainly wouldn't accept the truth, and she had left the scene, which would make her appear guilty.

Oh, Grandmother, tell me what to do. Please don't abandon me. She concentrated on visualizing New Orleans, her grandmother's home, and the smells and tastes that made that city home. She imagined long fingers reaching out into space grasping for a message from her grandmother. But she caught only air.

She heard steps coming down the street, and she turned her back to face a store window, an empty window of a jewelry store. She rested her forehead against the glass and waited for the traveler to pass. The footsteps stopped behind her and she glanced at the window to see the reflection. The person appeared to be a male. She couldn't make out the age or social status.

"May I help you, mademoiselle?"

She shook her head.

"Are you sure? It's very late and a young lady like you shouldn't be roaming the streets."

Again she shook her head.

"Mademoiselle, I really would prefer to see you home or at least to the nearby police station if you need help."

Furiously she turned to face the intruder.

"I don't need help. Go away."

"I don't mean to be too forward, but do you have someplace to stay?"

She realized she had simply thrown on some clothes and hadn't bothered to even comb her hair. She must look like a crazy woman, she thought.

"My boyfriend and I had a fight and I left in a huff. I really don't want to return right now."

"Then let me assist." The deep lines on his face softened when he smiled. "Why don't I take you to a place I know that is open all night. I can buy you some coffee and a bite to eat."

Her body relaxed as she looked into his blue eyes. After what she had experienced, kindness was the last gift she had expected from anyone.

"Perhaps I should find a place to sit and think," she said.

"Of course. Petty arguments between lovers are often forgotten in a day or two." He presented his arm to her and she accepted.

"Is the place far from here, monsieur?"

"Just several blocks away. My name is Arnaud, and yours?"

She hesitated, finding it difficult distinguishing herself from her grandmother. If she rejected her grandmother, she might never again be able to contact her.

"My name is Marie," she said, offering a smile of her own.

"Marie, you are not from Paris, are you?"

"No, I arrived only a short while ago."

"And this boyfriend, he's someone you recently met?"

Her body stiffened. Why did he want to know so much?

"I'm sorry, monsieur, I don't believe it is any of your business."

"You're right. I only thought to make conversation. But . . ."

He hesitated and she wondered why.

"I think you could use a friend. Your clothes are mismatched and wrinkled. It seems you may have need of some help."

"I told you. I hurried out of the apartment and didn't have a chance to . . ."

"And he didn't try to stop you or even chase after you?"

"Perhaps he doesn't love me as much as I thought."

The man nodded. "Down here, mademoiselle."

She stared down a long brick alleyway that led into a blackness in which she couldn't peer.

"But there's nothing down there, monsieur."

"You can't see it from here, but there's a turn at the end and there we'll find a delightful café. I go there frequently myself when I'm down in the dumps." He nudged her forward.

"No, monsieur, it is too dark."

"Trust me. I wouldn't harm you. I have daughters myself, not quite as old as you but close. You'll love the café. The owners are very good friends of mine."

"They can't do very much business in such a secluded location," she said.

"They're semiretired. It's a way for them to have a gathering place for their friends."

"Why can't they use their living room?"

"Please, don't ask any more questions. As you say, this area is quite desolate, so keep moving."

She felt the press of something against her ribs and looked down to see the blade in her companion's hand.

Chapter Forty-six

Marie Laveau sat on her balcony watching children play in the street. They pushed each other, fell, screamed, fought, and made up in short spaces of time. None seemed to hold a grudge. Most had known each other since they had played as babies. Their mothers had set examples for them, and each child relished being able to feel free in the midst of his or her peers.

Marie Laveau knew what grudges felt like. As an old woman she had dealt with many grudges. Some insults she forgave, especially those coming from people who mattered little to her. Forgiving a loved one, ah, that called for great understanding and strength on her part. When she loved, she set her trust in the return of a mutual caring. She didn't expect more than what a person seemed capable of doing, but she did anticipate that the other person would try the best they could to reciprocate her love.

She knew that at times she had disappointed some important people in her life, but she had done her best to make up for it. Her husband should have locked her out of their home after she left to stay with the vampire. Not only had she been unfaithful, she had also brought potential evil into her family's lives. What if Sade had had a taste for one of her girls? She knew now that he would have acted upon the attraction without hesitating. And now she had sent off her granddaughter to claim victory over a vicious vampire. Had she been too self-involved to see the potential danger?

Marie Laveau closed her eyes and prayed to the spirits for their intervention. Bring her home to me, she pleaded. I will never again send her away. Keep her safe from Sade.

She had been up all night attempting to recontact her granddaughter, but the spirits hadn't cooperated. Instead it seemed they punished her for the carelessness with which she had treated one so tender of age. A child still, she thought. Her granddaughter didn't have the experience nor the blackened heart of the real Marie Laveau.

Believers of vodoun knew that anyone who died from an unnatural magical death could be brought back as a zombie. She wondered whether she would be able to claim Sade's soul for her own uses. Already she had stolen his niece's soul from the ether, but Liliana had been confused and as a vampire, unable to free herself completely from the earth's bindings. Sade and his niece could aspire to the heavens, but they would never be welcomed. And neither would Marie Laveau. All her prayers to the saints and Masses for her soul wouldn't be able to expunge her sins.

But if I must go to hell, you will join me, Sade. I will surely arrive first, but you will eventually follow when the earth is finished.

Marie Laveau could only hope that Sade had not turned her granddaughter into one of the undead. A clean death with a slightly blemished soul would surely gain her granddaughter Heaven.

Let's go for a walk in the woods,
While the wolf is not there,
If the wolf were there, he would eat us.
Wolf, are you there?
Can you hear me?
What are you doing?

—French Nursery Rhyme

Chapter Forty-seven

Liliana had spent too long with her eyes shut. Now she opened them wide attempting to sight a person or object that could ground her. Everyone and everything around her whizzed by without her being able to make contact. Always being left behind would not do. She had to find her own way back to her uncle and not rely on chance. Chance merely limited her time with him, and often she sensed her surroundings weren't real. When her uncle visited her, the world would stop to allow her to touch, taste, smell, and even hear. Why, she wondered, would that be? Had someone invaded the world she shared with her uncle? Who?

She sensed animosity and also pain and a power too strong for her to fight. Or . . .

Maybe she hadn't tried hard enough to control herself. In her agony, despair flooded through her. Despair made her lethargic and vulnerable. All those memories she had been forced to acknowledge had lifted the catatonic state in which she had been trapped after she had been destroyed in the cemetery.

The world had been wonderful at one time. Could it possibly be so again? Had she abandoned the world, not the other way around?

Tiny sparks lit embers that quickly faded because she wouldn't allow the real world in. Opportunities to test herself frightened her too much.

How could her uncle have any interest in bringing back someone so useless as she? A wallflower. She hadn't been a wallflower in life, but in death she sat waiting, not trying. For what? For someone to reach across the border between life and death and pluck her out. And someone had.

Someone with evil intent. She had answered an unknown voice because she had been waiting.

Uncle, if I come to you on my own, will you accept me? Will you hug me and take joy in the reunion?

But how to slow it all down? How to quicken her step?

Someone used her to torture her uncle. Now she only existed as a dream for him. She troubled his sleep instead of bringing him peace. She loved her uncle, and wouldn't allow someone to pierce his heart in such a way any longer.

She moved closer to the blur before her. Sometimes she recognized shapes. A smell would occasionally break through the barrier making her remember a taste. Oh, and how her uncle's hands felt on her flesh, she especially felt joy in that.

"Stop!" she demanded, hearing her voice echo.

"Stop!" she screamed louder, but she only heard her own voice.

She walked into the blur surrounded by movement. Surrounded by life. She could hear breathing, the beating of hearts, and the breezes set in motion by those around her.

Next to her laughter broke out. But to the front she heard weeping, sad tears, not angry or fearful tears.

"Liliana. Come, Liliana."

She remained steady. The enemy called again. The voice that had tricked her into taunting her uncle.

"Liliana, it is time to visit with your uncle again. Don't you want to do that? I can bring you both together. He's waiting. Don't disappoint him."

She tried to concentrate on the world that whirled around her. The crying, the laughter faded. No, no, she pleaded, don't desert me when I need you the most.

"Liliana, don't be a bad girl. I can make it so that you'll never see your uncle again. Do you want that?"

If it would give him peace, yes, she would.

"Don't make me force you to come, Liliana. Remember the punishment I sent."

Liliana felt a knife digging into her heart. Her soul had been set afire. And more despair than she had ever felt washed away her will.

Sade sat on a rock in the middle of a wood. Was he waiting for her?

"Uncle," she said, moving into the clearing so that he could see her.

"You look tired, Liliana. Have you not been allowed to rest?"

"It's time I wake. Time that I take charge of myself again."

"How will you do that?"

"By actively seeking you out. Do you mind? We love . . ."

"No. I loved a child. A pretty little girl who could make me laugh and delighted in the slightest attention I paid her. You're not that girl. She's gone forever."

"Only because of laziness and hopelessness. But I can come back to you without the wicked person who forces these dreams upon you. And I will come while you're awake so that we can share time alone, no intruders to limit us."

"Liliana, I refuse to talk to the air."

"But I'm substance, Uncle. I have thoughts, desires, and love."

"You expect me to suffer daydreams of you."

"Do you hate me?"

"I loved Liliana. I will always love her memory. But you I detest."

"But I am Liliana. I have her memories, her beliefs, her feelings. Can't you see that same little girl in me?"

Laughter filled the air, misshaping the world around them.

"I hear a Vodou Queen who is purposefully taunting me with her magic."

"I'm not part of her magic. I'm . . ."

"No, you're not the child I played with. Not anymore. You're a pawn that's meant to destroy me." Sade paused for a moment. "You look so much like my Liliana, but there is no substance to you."

"I still exist, Uncle, independent of whatever has called me to consciousness. I will prove that to you and you will love me again."

Chapter Forty-eight

"Please don't, Liliana." Sade lay in his coffin, too tired to raise the lid, wishing he could go back to sleep, wishing he didn't have to push Liliana away.

He raised his hands and touched the quilted satin lining of his coffin. Gradually he lifted the lid until it rested back on its hinges. The dark room hovered over him, blaming him, cursing him. He sat and oriented himself for a few moments before descending from the coffin. The coldness of the marble floor jerked him fully awake. He wanted to sit and read for hours. He wanted to remain in France and continue his life as it had been before the dreams. One day he hoped to be able to think of Liliana without dread. But today he would leave for New Orleans to face the famous Vodou Queen who should have long been dead.

He had packed his suitcases and he had stored French soil in upstate New York; therefore, he would have to make a brief stop before continuing on to New Orleans.

He knew he would run into his mother-in-law in the

States. He'd be lucky if she hadn't booked the same flight as he. What the hell did she think she could do beyond wrecking his plans?

What should one take when visiting a Vodou Queen? he wondered. Rosaries? A cross? Ah, but she used those articles in her magic. She had prayed to Catholic saints and had attended Mass regularly. And probably still did. Her blend of religions had given her the ability to perform great magic. How honed were those powerful skills now? His soul didn't change into vapor the way Liliana's had. However, he recognized that she had managed to practice some sort of magic over him. Had she saved strands of his hair or clippings from his nails? Had she made herself a poppet that she poked with needles?

He knew that since Liliana had died an unnatural death, her soul would have been vulnerable. He had talked too much about his Liliana, but at the time she still existed and held sway over his heart. Marie Laveau knew of his love and at times expressed jealousy, but she never seemed threatening.

"How blind you were," he said, shaking his head remorsefully. "I failed you more than once, Liliana."

He'd dress in a business suit since he wanted to call as little attention as he could to himself. When he arrived in New Orleans, he had a place to stay on Bourbon Street over a seedy strip joint where he often found sustenance. The booze and the naked women muddled most of the men's heads making them easy prey.

He would find Marie Laveau in her old home. She had left her home only once, for him. He imagined she had never left it again after he had moved on.

Now she waited in that old home for him. What surprises would she have? Could she still want to be made into an immortal vampire? By now she must suffer from aging; otherwise she would not have sent a substitute to seduce him.

Soon you'll be able to confront me with all the rage and willpower you have. And you will lose again.

Chapter Forty-nine

She lay on the gurney mesmerized by the hospital lights that flooded the emergency room. The curtain had only partially been drawn around her. The voices sang out with terms she did not recognize, with numbers that meant nothing to her.

The granddaughter shivered with a chill. Her side felt wet and her shirt clung to her flesh. Her legs ached and the dried crust on her skin tightened her flesh.

Shivering badly, she tried to raise the top half of her body, but when she did, the pain in her side pierced her and caused more blood to flow.

Grandmother, I need you. Please save me.

"Who's the one in the corner? Anyone see to her yet?"

"A rape victim. Police brought her in about forty-five minutes ago but no one's had a second to check her over."

"Let's get to it. Looks like she's been bleeding a while."

She held her breath, afraid to be noticed and afraid she would die.

"She give a name?"

"Just some mumbling. No one's been able to understand her."

Someone pushed the curtain back, exposing the granddaughter.

"Mademoiselle, how are you doing? Can you understand me?"

She nodded her head and attempted to focus on the face that floated above her. The elderly man didn't look anything like her assailant. Age hadn't wrinkled his skin badly; instead, his face looked pasty white but smooth.

"What is your name, mademoiselle?"

She heard the stirring of sobs coming up from her chest.

"Do you know your name?"

The elderly man looked away and faced a nurse who stood at the foot of the gurney.

"Any head injury?"

"None was noted when she was brought in."

His faded gray eyes looked back at her. His hands began a search of her body starting with her head.

"Get some blankets for her. Quick with that."

He pulled the material away from her side and she winced.

"We need your name."

Who am I? she wondered. She remembered New Orleans, an old house, and an elaborate altar. There she retained the title Queen.

"Marie Laveau," she said.

"Do you remember what happened?"

"A man wanted to help me. He wanted . . ." She shook uncontrollably.

"Where are those damn blankets?" the man yelled.

Warm wool spilled across her body.

"Grandma," she yelled.

"Anyone call her family?"

"She had no identification on her and she's not very cooperative."

"How can we reach your grandmother, mademoiselle?" The elderly man stared at her again expecting an answer, but she felt sick.

What had she eaten? she asked herself. She didn't want to be ill. They had just put these clean blankets on her for warmth. If she were sick, they would take them away and she would be colder than ever.

"Hurry, get a pan. She's going to be sick."

She tried to roll to her side, but the pain briefly sent her into blackness. A split second later she recaptured the sound of voices. Her eyes filled with tears and her stomach muscles spasmed.

Hands raised up the top half of her body as she vomited. Sobbing and coughing, she tried to bat away the unfamiliar hands helping her. Too weak to succeed, she dropped her arms to her sides.

Chapter Fifty

The beat of the music came up through the floor and the shrill cries from the street poured through the open window. The room looked the same; nothing had been moved, although the maids had cleaned away the dust.

He checked the time when he heard the marching band moving through the street. Every evening at the same time the band played its rowdy tunes and the tourists tagged along like sheep. Some would peel off at Preservation Hall; others would singly or in pairs do the same at the local bars; those with perseverance would end up abandoned at the end of the march.

Sade slammed the window shut and pulled the shade. A dim twenty-five-watt bulb lit only a small portion of the room. The kitchenette and his crated coffin still remained in the dark.

He sat in a cherry leather chair, resting his feet on the matching ottoman. He wondered whether Marie Laveau could sense his presence in New Orleans. He reached out and picked up a book that had been resting on the side table. Since it was too dim to read, he merely leafed through the book, *The Serpent and the Rainbow*. He had read the book on the plane, and wondered whether the Haitian Vodou described in the book had any relationship to the vodou that Marie practiced.

He remembered the definition for hoodoo, "a variation of the word voodoo used commonly in the southern United States."

"Is that what you're practicing on Liliana and me?" he asked aloud. He flung the book on the floor and decided to eat.

New Orleans could never be described as subtle, Sade thought as he walked through the doors of the strip joint. Brash, bold, foolish, weird, and sometimes depressing described the city best.

A loud belch broke the beat of the music, and the dancer eased her way to the other side of the stage.

Sade sat at a table and ordered a drink. He had to ask for several brand names before the waitress was able to fill his order.

He heard the chair next to him squeak across the wood floor. A hand wiped the seat clean before a mature female sat. The woman definitely had passed her fiftieth birthday, but he guessed she hadn't yet reached sixty.

The waitress set his drink on the table.

"Elsa, I'll have my usual," said the woman.

The waitress looked at Sade and he nodded his head.

Feeling welcomed, the woman pulled her chair closer to the table and closer to Sade.

"I used to work here," she said.

He looked at her. "Recently?"

She cackled and nudged his arm with her elbow. Her old clothes fit her poorly and the mismatched colors made her look like a Goodwill reject. Her rouged cheeks flushed even more with her delight, and her lipstick-stained teeth were crooked.

"I wish. It paid a hell of a lot better than what I do now." The woman's drink arrived and she paused to take a swig. "See this blouse?" Her hands grabbed onto the material and stretched it out. "I used to fill this up." She formed two little peaks where her nipples should be. She dropped the material to take another drink. "Lost thirty pounds the past couple of months. Can't seem to stop losing."

"You should seek medical help, madam."

"Hmmm. 'Madam' sounds like I run a whorehouse. I'm not that lucky either. I work at Wal-Mart. I'm the one with the price gun going 'smack, smack, smack,'" she said, hitting his arm in example.

Sade removed his arm from the table and rested his hand on the back of her chair.

"Touchy, touchy," she said. "Hey, you got a real French accent or is it Cajun?"

"I've only just arrived from Paris, madam."

"New York or France?" She smacked his chest with the back of her left hand. When he didn't respond, she continued. "There is a Paris, New York, you know."

He nodded.

"What you here for?" she asked. "You don't seem interested in the show and you look like you could afford a high-priced girl."

"I came in to unwind and imbibe," he said.

"You ain't touched your drink yet so you can't be that thirsty."

"Ah, but I am." He moved closer to her.

"Can I have another?" she said, pointing at her empty glass.

He caught the eye of the waitress, who immediately came over.

"Another glass of . . ."

"She's not allowed more than two drinks, mister."

"Ah, El, you're not going to get smart-assed with me tonight?"

"Maggie, I've already gone over your limit and if the boss finds out I'll lose my job."

The woman stood and took a deep breath.

"You bitch," she screamed.

Sade pulled on the sleeve of her blouse to catch her attention.

"Madam, I'm sure we can go someplace else for a drink." The waitress swiftly moved away from the table. "Perhaps even go up to my room."

"None of that stuff. I'm finished with spreading my legs for booze. The president of Wal-Mart would be shocked to hear one of his stock clerks was diving into bed with every Tom, Dick, and Harry."

"I'm Louis."

"Ah, that's different," she said, giving out with a grating cackle. Again she swept the back of her hand against Sade's chest. "At least I still got my sense of humor," she muttered, picking up the empty glass to drain the last drop.

"There's no shortage of bars on Bourbon Street, madam. Shall we move on to a fresher location?" He threw several big bills on the table.

"I was right. You got lots of the green."

He stood and reached to take her arm, but she pulled away.

"What you want with me?"

"Company," he said.

"You could find younger and more attractive company, so why get stuck with me?"

"Madam, you're easy. I can sit and chat with you and who knows, I might get lucky at the end of the night. I'm not in the mood for playing games."

"That's sure straightforward," she said. "You got booze in your room?"

"Champagne."

She shook her head. "The bubbles give me gas. Any whiskey?"

"Several brands, and I have tonic water in case you care for a mixed drink."

"No fun in that. How far away is this room?"

"Right upstairs."

Chapter Fifty-one

Sex with Maggie hadn't appealed to Sade, so he waited for her to pass out and then took his nourishment. When she woke the next day, he offered to walk her home but she refused. He thought she couldn't make up her mind whether they had sex and if not, why not. Her embarrassment showed in her shaky hands and stuttered speech. Actually, she had spoken better when drunk.

Maggie checked her purse as a knock came from the front door. Sade and she stayed perfectly still.

"Louis," a familiar voice called.

Maggie looked at Sade and he shrugged. She began rubbing her neck, and opened the wounds from the night before, carrying blood away on her hand. He feared she might pass out when she saw the blood, but instead she ran to the sink to wash off her hand.

"Is that your girlfriend?" Maggie asked in a loud whisper.

He shook his head. "Mother-in-law," he replied in an even tone.

Maggie grabbed hold of the edge of the sink.

"Mother-in-law? I ain't never run into one of those."

The knocking became more insistent.

"Shit! Is there another way out of here?" Maggie asked.

He shook his head.

"Listen, I don't want to get involved in this. I only meant to share some company and a few drinks. Working at Wal-Mart doesn't give me much money for drinking and eating. Maybe you could go out there and talk to her and I could sneak by when she's not looking?"

Sade sighed, walked to the door, and opened it wide allowing Marie to rush in.

Maggie let out a little yelp.

"I didn't know about a wife. Honest. He don't wear any ring," Maggie defended.

"Why should he?" said Marie, waving Maggie toward the open door.

Maggie wasted no time in running for the door, and Sade and Marie could hear Maggie continue to tromp down the stairs.

"Louis! She's hardly your style."

"I felt sorry for her because she works at Wal-Mart." He slammed the door shut.

He briefly left Marie speechless.

"Pity? You've never pitied anyone and what does Wal-Mart . . ."

"Marie, I haven't located Marie Laveau as yet."

"But you do have some sense of where to find her."

"I assume she remains in the same house she's lived in for over a century."

"What are you going to do when you find her?"

"I don't know. My theory is that she wants to confront me. That's as far as I've gone with this plan."

"You could be walking into a trap."

"I doubt she'll be hiding behind her front door with a stake in her hand."

"Then what does she want?"

"Control. She's proving she can control me."

"Think she'll attempt to make you a zombie?"

"What good would I be to her as a zombie?"

"She'd have complete control over you."

"What fun is it to control a drooling moron?"

"Why involve Liliana?"

"Only one person could force me to face Marie Laveau."

"Does she know the truth about Liliana?"

"Marie, I have never told anyone. Only you and I know."

"And what if Liliana learns she is your daughter? What if somehow you reveal this information in one of those dreams?"

Lie there, lie there, you false-hearted man,
Lie there instead of me;
Six pretty maidens have you drowned here,
And the seventh has drowned thee.

—Anonymous

Chapter Fifty-two

Liliana would charm her uncle back into her life. He could never resist his smallest, prettiest, and—she chuckled—only niece. He had spoiled her, never had scolded her, well, hardly ever, and had always fallen victim to her whims.

She had known no father besides the vague stories told to her. She hadn't even been able to draw out a good description of him from her grandparents. Instead, they'd reacted with anger. They'd left her with the impression that he had been a rogue who had wronged their daughter.

"Was he a highwayman?" she had asked.

Her grandparents had squeezed their faces into ugly contortions and shaken their heads.

"Was he wealthy?" she had asked.

And they'd looked to the ceiling.

"There must be something you can tell me about how he looked, what he did, his background."

"Go to sleep. Someday you will understand."

But she never had. Although she had never tired of asking.

Her uncle's wife, sister to her own mother, shied away from Liliana. Never mean, her aunt managed to always be preoccupied. Liliana found herself rarely invited to her uncle's chateau, and when she did go, her aunt would flee with her own children.

But Uncle made time for her. He took her riding and showed her the sights of Paris, all the marvelous children's plays and wonderful amusement rides.

Never had she questioned why her uncle paid her so much attention. She had taken his being smitten with her for granted. No more, though. Now that he had rejected her, she wondered why.

"Uncle, dear Uncle, take me back into your arms." She reached out for him but didn't find him.

How does that wicked woman control us? she wondered. Does she steal into our hearts only to rip them apart?

"I love you, Uncle. No one else has meant so much to me."

He knew how to comfort her when fear took away her breath.

"Wretched crone, come again and I will steal your secret. I'll lull you into trusting me."

How long would she have to wait?

"Where are you?" she screamed. "Take me to my uncle. Let him remember his love for me."

"Calm yourself, child." The ancient voice came from all around Liliana. "I have my own precious child to find."

"May I help you, old woman?"

"Why would you want to do that?"

"We can help each other," Liliana said.

"There's nothing you can do for me except play havoc with Sade's mind. Ah . . ."

"Yes?" Liliana waited several minutes in silence.

"You can ask him a question."

"And what is that question?"

"Ask him what he did with Marie Laveau in Paris."

"If you bring him to me I will ask the question. I promise."

The old voice turned into a laugh.

"Liliana."

She turned, and her uncle stood within two feet of her. She wanted to enfold him in a hug but didn't dare.

"Seems you'll never be rid of me, Uncle."

"She forces us. . . ."

"No, I asked to see you."

"Foolish girl. You have nothing to gain except pain."

"More than pain. I have bartered with this woman who hates you."

"What do you have to give her?"

"She wants to know what you did with Marie Laveau in Paris."

He smiled. "The same thing I would have done with any beautiful woman."

"But does she live, uncle? I believe that is what she needs to know."

"She's with us now, Liliana. Eavesdropping. Plotting. Thinking she'll end up the winner."

"Is she one of us?"

"Wanted to be."

"You refused so she seeks to punish us."

"I have a question for her. Who was that young woman, Marie Laveau, really? She looked like you, but when I touched her I was sure it was not you. She's weak, unstable. And the gris-gris you gave her is gone. But you must know that, Marie Laveau. Is she one of your walking zombies?"

Liliana felt the air quiver around her. She began to fall out of her uncle's dream. No, no, hold on, she whispered to herself. *Don't be tossed away so easily.*

"Uncle, stay with me." She reached out to her uncle's fading shape and watched as he turned his back on her.

Chapter Fifty-three

"I want to go with you, Louis. You owe me this. You ruined both my daughters' lives and stole my granddaughter from me. I want to know what this Marie Laveau wants."

"Marie, there is no reason for you to come. You do not know this woman, and you may put Liliana into more danger."

"How? By trying to reason with this Vodou Queen?"

"Reason?" Sade burst into laughter.

"If you don't take me with you, I'll follow. Imagine how much trouble I can cause if you don't know exactly where I am or what I'm doing."

"Come, Marie, but I won't protect you. The Vodou Queen has an enormous amount of power. She must to overcome Liliana's and my wills."

"I don't ask for anything from you, Louis. I'm going for my granddaughter, not for you."

The pair exited the building together and joined a crowd of tourists. They made an odd couple, Louis with his hair hanging straight beyond his shoulders, Marie in typical dominatrix attire. But in New Orleans no one took any notice of them except for a drunken conventioneer, who quickly learned the penalty for touching Marie's net-covered thigh.

"Did you see what that fool did, Louis?"

"No more foolish than your knocking him down in the middle of a crowded street." He turned right into a narrow street lined with homes badly in need of repair. He stopped in front of one that he remembered.

"This is her house?" Marie asked.

"This is where she and I lived centuries ago."

"Don't dawdle. How can you even consider walking down memory lane? Where the hell does this Vodou Queen live?"

"See the window on the top floor, the one to the right?"

"The one with the sheet spread across it?"

"Yes." He looked at Marie. "We shared that apartment. The heat in that apartment would have been oppressive except that I'm not human. Poor Marie Laveau would be covered with perspiration most of the day, but she never complained."

"She had you. What did she have to complain about?" Marie smiled sweetly at him.

"This isn't a joke, Marie. I must remember our time together, the words we spoke, the feelings expressed, and the vulnerabilities she had."

"Get on with it, Louis, and stop being melodramatic." Marie's face hardened. The smile disappeared completely.

Sade nodded and continued down the street, making several more turns before arriving at Marie Laveau's home.

"The place is decrepit. Are you sure someone still lives here?"

"The doors leading out onto the upper balcony are open. I believe she awaits me. You may be a surprise."

"Do we knock or force the door?"

"Marie, you are not subtle at all. We should knock obviously."

"Unless we want to catch her off guard."

"No, she knows I am here. I imagine a withered old woman rocking in her chair, drinking some nasty brew from a skull." He looked at Marie and touched her head.

"Too many apertures, as you should well know."

"Yes." His eyes looked beyond Marie to the time when he had carried around her skull inside his own coffin. A time of peace, as he recalled, until . . .

"Louis, wake up. Are you in one of the dreams?"

"No, just a pleasant reverie." He walked to the front door and reached for the odd-shaped knocker that had been used so much it no longer retained its original shape. He pounded the knocker against the door several times and waited. There was no sound coming from within the building.

"Maybe you're wrong," Marie said.

"No. It must be difficult for her to get around." He left Marie at the door and went back onto the street.

An old woman stood on the balcony, her hair covered with a brown tignon, her clothes massive on her slight body. The wrinkles on the face hid the features, and he could see that she had a humped back even though she attempted to stand tall.

"Marie Laveau, you've called for me and I am here." He gave a gentlemanly bow.

She raised her hand and beckoned him to come in.

Unable to contain herself, his mother-in-law hurried to his side.

He saw the Vodou Queen's eyes squint, and she sniffed the air like a bloodhound.

"Who do you bring with you, my love?"

Sade didn't get a chance to answer.

"I too am a Marie, madam. I am Liliana's grandmother." Marie pushed herself in front of Sade, forcing him to trip on the curb.

"I know your pain, Grandmother, for I too have a granddaughter. Come in, both of you, and we can share our sad stories," Marie Laveau said.

Chapter Fifty-four

"There has been some serious damage done to your reproductive system, mademoiselle. I'm afraid you will never be able to bear your own children."

"But I must continue the name. The magic can't stop with me," the granddaughter said.

"Magic, mademoiselle?"

"I am Marie Laveau, Vodou Queen of New Orleans. You must know me."

"No, mademoiselle, I don't. We'll be keeping you for a few days. . . ."

"No! I must go home today. He will return looking for me."

"Who?"

"The Marquis de Sade."

She saw the elderly doctor frown.

"Mademoiselle, I'd like you to speak with a colleague who may be able to help you. It seems you may be a bit confused."

The granddaughter raised herself to a seated position and looked around the room. She saw at least five other beds, but only half were occupied. The blinds were pulled up and she could see the Eiffel Tower in the distance.

Turning back to the doctor, she reached out and took his hand.

"I am well. I'm expected back home."

"Allow us to contact your family and . . ."

"I'm Marie Laveau," she reiterated. "I'm the last Marie Laveau," she said, recalling what the doctor had told her. "There'll never be another. She'll be very disappointed when I tell her."

"Tell who, mademoiselle?"

"When I tell the dead Vodou Queen that I'll not be able to pass on the charms and magic."

"I strongly suggest you speak with my colleague, Doctor—"

"No!" She attempted to swing her feet off the bed and onto the floor, but the pain in her side blinded her.

"The wound is not serious, mademoiselle, but given the location it will be quite painful for a while."

"Doctor, the psychiatrist said he wouldn't be able to see her until late this afternoon," a nurse said, interrupting.

"Psychiatrist? But I'm not mad."

"You've suffered several serious traumas. I think it would be good to speak to someone in the field," said, the doctor.

"My clothes?" the granddaughter asked.

"They weren't salvageable. We'll need to send someone to your place for a change of clothes."

"Don't do that." She hadn't let go of the doctor's hand, and now she gripped it with all her might. "Please, buy me some new clothes or give me used clothes. Clothing left by the dead will even do."

She watched the doctor turn to the nurse, who shrugged her shoulders. He turned back to the patient.

"Mademoiselle, there was no identification on you. Do you have a home?"

She pulled back her hand and eased her legs back onto the mattress.

"Of course. My home is in New Orleans."

"But here in Paris, mademoiselle, where have you been staying?"

She lay back on her pillows. "I'm tired."

The doctor sighed.

"I could see if another psychiatrist is available," said the nurse.

"We can't force her to stay." The doctor reached into his pants pocket and pulled out some euros. "Get her some clothes. I don't want her wandering the streets in her hospital gown."

The nurse nodded.

"Mademoiselle, you can always come back to the hospital and ask for me." He gave her his card. "If I'm not here, the hospital staff knows how to reach me."

"Thank you, Doctor. I'll be fine."

She could see that he didn't believe her, but he turned away followed closely by the nurse, who paused at the door.

"Mademoiselle, your size?"

. . . Where earth and ocean meet,
And all things seem only one
In the universal sun.

—Percy Bysshe Shelley

Chapter Fifty-five

Liliana listened to the world again. She didn't capture every sound, but the few words, songs, sighs, and noises that she understood gave her hope. Her world had been quiet for a long time. Now she recognized barks, babes crying, and a strong voice. He asked for admittance.

"Of course, of course," she cried, but he didn't listen. Instead he called out to a woman she didn't know. A woman who chose to speak to her.

"Liliana, I have him now. He is here. Can you hear his footsteps on the stairs?"

Liliana remained very still. Ah, yes, she could hear footsteps coming near. Confident steps. Familiar steps. But they echoed with another's. A lighter step, a feminine step that followed him.

"Yes, Liliana. Your grandmother comes too. She wants you back as much as I want my granddaughter back. A trade. Can we manage a fair exchange, one lifeless soul for one that reverberates with life? I hold you tight against me, Liliana. I cannot afford for your wisp of a soul to fly away from me."

A hand grasped Liliana tightly, but gentleness cushioned the hold and Liliana rested in the warmth.

A door creaked and the footsteps came closer.

"Uncle," Liliana whispered. "Uncle, can you feel my presence?"

"He knows you cannot be far from me. My power fills the room in which he stands and makes your poor grandmother dizzy on her feet."

The voice laughed, enjoying the control.

Liliana listened hard, but a higher-pitched voice drowned out the sound of her dear uncle's words.

She tried to shush the extra person, but realized no one except the mistress controlling her soul could hear her.

"I'll take great care of you, Liliana, for I want my own flesh and blood back. He looks tired, Liliana, we have kept him from his sleep for too long. His complexion is sallow, his gait isn't as strong as I remembered. His eyes have faded into a lighter blue and his cheeks show no sign of the blood he has stolen. Still, he retains his charismatic charm that makes men and women strip naked to bare their flesh for the touch of his whip. He is far from finished, Liliana. And he still loves you for why else would he be here? He warns you away from him, but his love for you makes him weak."

"I don't want him to suffer because of me."

"He will always suffer because of you, Liliana. He doesn't know it. He tries to hide from the love he feels, but he'll never escape it. Settle deeper into my clutches, little dove. Don't fly away ever. Be with me and you will know his true touch once again."

"How can that be if I don't have a body?"

"Feel through my hands, luxuriate in his touch of my flesh, see him as I do, and smell the scent of his death through me."

"But that is nothing like being true substance. I don't want to cry through your tears nor feel him through your touch. Give me flesh once again."

Chapter Fifty-six

Sade's mother-in-law stared at the cluttered room. Stacked jars leaned dangerously forward on the china cabinet. Throw rugs overlapped all across the wooden floor. The ancient velvet drapes glistened with their age. Several human skulls lay casually piled on the floor at the foot of a table decorated with colorful fabrics and strange statues.

The woman in the rocking chair could have been mistaken for death itself. The terrarium on the low table next to the rocking chair contained a small snake that slithered slowly back and forth.

"What a disgusting creature," Marie said, pointing at the terrarium.

"Careful. Hope will certainly take offense on behalf of her sister," said the Vodou Queen.

"Marie, don't move. There's another snake behind you. Only this one's not enclosed in a container," Sade said, taking the arm of his mother-in-law.

She looked down to find a snake sliding through her legs in its attempt to cross the room to the Vodou Queen.

"Louis, I'm not happy."

"And I didn't ask you to come."

Hope curled up at the feet of the Vodou Queen.

"It is rare for Hope to come out in front of strangers, but Sade, you are no stranger to her. She has been with us when we have made love."

"I assure you that I was never aware of Hope's company."

"How do I look, Sade? Can you still see my beauty? Can you even recognize me after all these years?" the Vodou Queen asked.

"I almost didn't recognize your granddaughter in Paris. She is your granddaughter, *oui*?"

"You speak in the present so I can assume she is still alive. Is she still mortal?"

"*Oui*. Did you expect me to give her the vampire life?"

"I hoped you hadn't. You look surprised, Sade. I don't want my granddaughter feeding off the innocent. She is too delicate for that life. I, on the other hand, would have made an enchantingly wise vampire. But now, sadly, it is too late. I would have difficulty overcoming my prey and what sense is there in keeping this worn body alive?"

"You've waited only for me to come back?"

"And it has taken too long. Although you may feel that it hasn't been long enough." The Vodou Queen lifted Hope into her arms. "Sit," she said, indicating the love seat within a few feet of her.

"He doesn't have time to dally, crone. We're here to free Liliana's soul," Marie said.

"And how will you do that?" the Vodou Queen asked.

Marie took a step forward, but Sade pulled her back.

The Vodou Queen rested her back against the spokes of the rocking chair and closed her eyes. "She's with us, you know. She has many questions, many fears. It is hard for me to keep her quiet."

"Then let her speak," said Sade.

Marie Laveau opened her eyes.

"Do you really want to hear her questions and accusations? She has no joy, Sade, beyond you. Poor Liliana is obsessed with her uncle. Her kind, gentle, sweet uncle. She doesn't even sense the presence of her grandmother. Why is that? Why could an uncle mean so much more to her than a grandmother?"

"That's because he's her father," Marie blurted out.

The Vodou Queen grabbed her midsection and fought for air.

Sade turned to his mother-in-law and grabbed her shoulders.

"You fool, whatever you tell this witch, Liliana hears."

"She should know. She always should have known. We did no favors by lying to her. I thought I could protect her from you, but I'm an idiot not to understand that there would be an invisible bond between you and Liliana. You two fawned over each other. If you were nearby she would find you. If she were upset you would call at our house."

"No more an uncle," the old woman hissed. "Go, both of you."

"We won't go until you free Liliana," Marie yelled, seeing the large snake rear up its head.

"I need to talk to Liliana, Marie Laveau. I must calm her," implored Sade.

The crone shook her head and pointed toward the door.

"She'll not rest until I can explain."

"She'll never rest, Sade. She'll writhe and cry forever."

"And your granddaughter. Where is she?" he asked.

"She'll come back to me."

"I destroyed the gris-gris you gave her. She is without protection. You can't connect to her, can you? That's why you didn't know whether she was dead or alive or even a vampire. Give us Liliana and I'll go find your granddaughter."

Marie watched Louis and the old Vodou Queen stare each other down. The old woman bit her hand, drawing blood with the pain she felt. She closed her eyes and her lips moved, but she didn't say a word.

"Louis, Liliana must be fighting for control. Liliana can't take this crone's body because she'd be trapped in a nightmare. Stop her."

"You said the words that led to this. Can you take back your words?" he asked Marie.

"Of course not, what point are you making?"

"I am not the cause. . . ."

"You are the leper spreading the plague, Louis."

Louis turned away and walked to the door.

"Where the hell are you going?" Marie screamed. "Our baby is trapped inside this filthy beast and you're walking away. You can't." Marie leaped forward and caught hold of Sade, pulling him back into the room.

"I can't face her, don't you understand? I've done too much harm. She is better off trapped inside a crone than haunting me."

"You are better off, Louis, not your daughter. You bedded your wife's sister, caring nothing about the consequences. When you learned my baby was pregnant, you ran to your wife for comfort and the fool took you back.

After the baby was born, you doted on the infant but refused to even speak to the mother. She died loving you, Louis. Died loving a man who could never love."

"But he does love." The weak voice of the crone interrupted the fight. "He loves the baby. His baby. Liliana. And I have her." Gripping the arms of her rocking chair, the crone stood on unsteady legs. "You, Sade, threw Liliana away and I took her."

"You putrefied corpse, you'll never see your granddaughter again." Sade freed himself from Marie's hold and quickly exited the house.

"Why make an innocent suffer?" Marie asked, moving toward the Vodou Queen.

"She can't be innocent if she comes from Sade's loins. She shares his sins merely by calling him father."

Hope reached out and tested the air with her forked tongue.

"I could rip you apart, then she would be free," Marie said.

"Would she, Grandmother? Would she?"

Chapter Fifty-seven

"As I said before, mademoiselle, I would prefer you not leave the hospital so soon."

"You would rather I talk to one of your psychiatrists so you could commit me." The granddaughter had dressed in the simple, cheap clothes the nurse had given her. Dressing had been painful, but she didn't dare stay. She would head for her apartment to pick up a few things including her money and passport. The dread of what awaited her in the apartment soured her stomach.

"Where will you go, mademoiselle?"

"Home to New Orleans."

"The police will want to talk to you."

"Have you reported this already?"

"We had to, but I'm not a jailer. I will not stop you from leaving."

"So far, Doctor, you've been very generous. Do you think you could help me out further with cab fare?"

"You take advantage of my pity for you," he said, reaching into his pocket.

"Sad that I must depend on your pity. I have your card, I'll send the money back."

"I'd prefer that you bring the money in person, mademoiselle."

The granddaughter winced.

"I'll give you some medication and a form for a renewal before you go. Will you be able to afford to buy the medicine I'll prescribe?"

"Give me enough medicine for the next few days. When I'm back in New Orleans my grandmother will be able to care for me."

"Is she a medical doctor?"

"She knows more about the art of curing than any doctor."

"Please see an internist when you get home, mademoiselle. Your grandmother may have helped you through many childhood illnesses, but this is far more serious. You will want to make sure your internal injuries are healing properly." He took her right hand, giving her more than enough money for a cab home.

"*Merci.*" She took the money and checked the bed and night table to make sure she hadn't left anything behind. At the nurses' station she picked up a paper bag containing the drugs the doctor had promised.

She walked as quickly as she could out of the hospital. The police would surely show up at the hospital sometime today, and she didn't want to answer any questions.

A nurse had called her a cab, and it waited just out front. She figured the driver would report back the address, but she'd be gone by the time the police tracked her down and hopefully flying home. She didn't ask the cab to wait; instead, she would call a new cab to take her to the airport. No sense allowing the authorities to know her every move.

She walked up several flights of stairs checking each new floor cautiously before continuing her climb. There was no indication that anyone had been in her apartment, and the body hadn't started to smell yet. Slowly she unlocked and opened her door just wide enough to squeeze herself into the apartment.

She had left the lights on. The living room showed no sign of the disaster in the bedroom. She wished she hadn't kept her money and credit cards in the bedroom. But she mustn't waste time. She moved directly toward the bedroom door, which stood ajar. She hadn't remembered closing or leaving the door open. Could the body now be a vampire, and if so what should she do? She changed directions and went to the kitchen. From a cupboard she pulled out a broom. She broke it across the kitchen table and tried to form a strong point on the end. She stood still for a couple of minutes just listening to the silence.

Daylight poured in through the kitchen window giving her some sense of security, but not enough to prevent her hands from shaking. The prostitute, if she were a vampire, would probably be weak, in need of blood and the night's camouflage.

The granddaughter moved quietly through the apartment until she reached the bedroom door. Here she stopped to take several breaths before pushing the door open.

Her side hurt. She should have taken another dose of

her pills while in the kitchen, but she had been afraid that it would slow her reflexes.

Inching her way into the room, she looked to her right and left making sure no one surprised her. Sprawled across the floor, the bloodless body hadn't moved or been moved. The prostitute would have had to have shared Sade's blood in order to become a vampire, and she never saw Sade offer of himself.

An unsavory smell filled the bedroom, but hadn't reached much farther into the apartment.

She grabbed an overnight bag and threw in a few personal items before opening the drawer of the bureau to take out her passport, money, and credit cards.

She peered over the foot of the bed to check on the body. Nothing moved. After setting the overnight bag and her purse outside the bedroom, she returned with the pointed end of the broomstick.

A groan issued from the mouth of the prostitute. Probably simply a death rattle, she told herself, but to make sure, she raised the broomstick high into the air and buried the sharpened end in the prostitute's heart.

At evening when the lamp is lit,
Around the fire my parents sit;
They sit at home and talk and sing,
And do not play at anything.

—Robert Louis Stevenson

Chapter Fifty-eight

Grandmother and Uncle must be playing at some game with this woman who holds me captive. There cannot be truth to the words Grandmother spoke. They never would have hidden such a secret joy from me, knowing how often I questioned them about my birth parents.

Liliana heard the beating of a heart. Not her own heart. No, she did not have a heart. Instead, the beat must come from the woman who grasped Liliana's soul in her hand. The weak beat skipped occasionally, but forcefully came back. This woman had much to do yet before she allowed her body to die.

"You heard the words your grandmother spoke, Liliana. I know they deeply hurt you. Your pain and shock doubled over my own body into the dread you felt. What do you want now, Liliana? What do you want now that you know your father abandoned you?"

Liliana's spirit shrank into a small ball, curling in on itself, taking up less and less space with each passing second.

"Tell me what you think of your father. Tell me how you can let your uncle go and replace him so easily with a man who rejected his own flesh."

Some would shriek with joy, some would weep in sadness, some would fester seeking revenge, but Liliana calmly tried to disappear. She sought the blankness of an empty hole in which nothing existed. This is what would save her from madness. Save her from being unloved.

Yet she couldn't find this vacuum. Couldn't make herself small enough not to exist. A trace of her would always exist whether her uncle were her father or not.

"His seed gave life to you but his self-love stole your rights away. I would call him to us to face you, but he dares not sleep."

"He wouldn't hide from me."

"Sade has spent your lifetime hiding from you. Hiding his secret sin, his secret sorrow."

"Bring him to me now," Liliana whispered, feeling her soul unfolding from a twisted ball.

"What good would it do either of us?"

"You could watch him squirm," Liliana said.

"But that is not why you want to contact him. I am not such a fool as to believe that."

"I wish to speak to my father."

"You have none."

"Let me speak to my uncle then."

Liliana's jailer laughed.

"What will you do with us now that you know the truth, old woman?"

"Sade made . . ." The voice faltered. "I cannot call what we did making love. Sade and I had sex. Glorious, free-spirited sex. He made me believe that there must be some love there or he could not treat me as intimately as he did. He talked often of you, Liliana. And I grew jealous. He would describe you as if you stood before us. I hated you without knowing you. Hated your warmth, your speech, your mannerisms, and most of all your closeness to him. How could such a young girl impress him so when she seemed almost innocent? As to the girl being his niece, I figured he had bedded you and called you niece to cover the long stays together. Now it is worse than I thought. You and he truly are connected."

"You envy me that?"

In the silence Liliana heard the jailer's breath heave, the heart slacken and pick up again, and she almost heard a sob.

"I could live all these years believing he had never loved," the voice continued. "His heart made of ice, his soul black from having never known love's torture, never having had to sacrifice. But he had been reachable. He had cared for a young babe, a young child, a young woman, and his love grew with every year she lived."

"I no longer am alive. Do you think his love is dwindling?"

"For him you will always exist. The rest of us pass through his life as marionettes providing him with a play, with distraction to pass his days."

"Take me to him."

"So you can lick each other's wounds and beat your breasts for all the lost time you can't make up?"

"But you wanted him to come to you."

"I wanted him to suffer. I wanted him to see what his callousness had left behind. There would be a drop of love left for me that would set his guilt afire. Instead, I've only brought myself pain."

"Free us!"

"Never. As long as I live you both will only be able to dream of each other. When I die you will return to nothing and he will accept that you are gone."

Chapter Fifty-nine

Marie pushed through the rowdy crowd, jerking away from unsuitable suitors and tossing the confused to the side. She and Sade hadn't been able to achieve their goal. Her granddaughter still remained bound in Marie Laveau's web. Louis had to return and fight for Liliana. She wouldn't let him give up.

Howls of laughter, and off-tune voices sang out bawdy songs in the strip joint in Sade's building. Some fools trying to mask their agony, she guessed.

She almost climbed the stairs, but stopped before her foot could touch the bottom step. Were they singing "La Marseillaise"?

The door to the strip joint stayed shut under her gentle push. When she slammed the door open, she knocked a brawny male to the floor. The place smelled of cheap booze, sweat, and a hint of semen. Several strippers stood on stage not knowing how to dance to a national anthem. The men didn't care as long as they got to stare.

Sade stood in the middle of the room, a bottle of champagne in one hand and a beer glass in the other. Ugh, she thought, he had ruined the champagne.

"You next up?" A man grabbed hold of Marie and carried her to the stage. The naked women on stage looked puzzled, but made room for her.

Eagerly, Marie took center stage and glared out at Louis. He didn't seem to notice until he heard the groundswell of "Take it off, babe." He looked like he would be sick as soon as their eyes made contact.

Louis didn't bother to pour more champagne into his half-filled glass; instead, he drank straight from the bottle to the cheers of his many fans.

When he finished, he dropped the bottle and glass to the floor.

"Excuse me, monsieur, but I must be on my way," he muttered to the owner, who had wrapped his arms across Sade's back.

"Ah, but stay. You've brightened up the place."

The surrounding group of men yelled in agreement.

Marie had made her way through the crowd, and could almost touch Sade's arm. She watched Sade purposely push another man into her arms.

"You lout," she yelled. Upon her next glance, she noticed Sade slipping out the door. "Get out of my way, you fools."

"Excuse me, lady. I'm the owner and we don't allow spontaneous stripping in here. If you come back on . . ."

"Idiot," she said, and fought her way to the door.

"Don't you want to know what days are tryout days, lady?" the owner called after her, and the crowd roared with laughter.

Once outside, she wondered whether she could be lucky enough to have Sade trapped inside his apartment.

The door to his apartment stood open. A loud racket came from the bedroom. She found Sade pulling out drawers and packing clothes into his suitcases.

"What are you doing? You can't run away."

He paused to glare at her.

"I'm going back to Paris to find Marie Laveau's granddaughter." He threw a shirt into a suitcase without folding it.

"Why the hell would she be in Paris? She must know that you'd come looking for her grandmother. You think she'd sit in Paris and wait for your return? Louis, you told me you left her with a dead body. Either she's in jail or on a plane headed here. Even without the magical gris-gris, she can figure out which scenario is better."

Sade fell into a pale, overstuffed chair.

"What should I do, Marie? I am exhausted."

Marie sat on the bed. Sade used his fingertips to massage his temples. He rubbed so hard that a rash began to form. His long hair looked stringy and he bit his bottom lip.

He dropped his hands onto the arms of the chair and squinted at Marie.

"The Vodou Queen stole my child. I must find her offspring and rip her throat out."

"Will you kill her or change her into a vampire?"

"Depends on my self-control."

"If she were one of us, her grandmother would cry."

"If she were one of us, Marie Laveau would live forever."

"Not a simple choice, Louis. Either way, I don't think

we'll free Liliana. What if Liliana takes the crone's body?"

"We destroy her."

"Because you don't want to smell the sour breath of an old woman or because you're still going to try to forget your daughter?"

"I don't want to love again. That's why I keep you around, Marie, to remind me of what hate feels like."

Chapter Sixty

"Your seat belt, mademoiselle."

The granddaughter looked up into the young face of a stewardess forcing her to recall what she needed to do. She searched for the two ends of the seat belt and locked them together.

As she had bustled through the airport, she had worried that a policeman would stop her either for committing murder or trying to leave without pressing charges against an unknown rapist.

"This your first time flying?" the man to her right asked.

"No, monsieur."

"You look nervous, that's why I asked."

"I'm fine. I had been rushing and feared I would miss the flight."

He laughed. "When do flights get off on time?"

She gave him a weak smile.

"Are you staying in New York?"

"No." She hesitated, wondering whether she should tell him the truth. Why not? "I'm going on to New Orleans."

"That home for you?"

"Always has been."

"Strange place. Must be weird growing up there." His brown eyes looked at her intently, waiting for not only the plane but the conversation to get off the ground.

"I love New Orleans, monsieur, or else I would not live there."

"Some people stay in cities for family reasons. Your family there?"

She decided to ignore him. Finally, he picked up the in-flight magazine and started to browse.

Family. Only her grandmother. Her relatives had left New Orleans, some because they shared the Laveau name, others because they wanted to abandon the old religion. Her own mother had gone to Haiti. She hadn't wanted to compete with the real Marie Laveau and had wanted to learn more about vodou. Some blamed an overdose of D-tubocurarine for the death. Her grandmother said her mother had a weak heart and couldn't contain a *vodon loa* or spirit.

"Could a baka, *an evil spirit in the form of an animal, have invaded the ceremony and killed Mother?"*

"Child, your mother couldn't learn from me. Careless and frivolous, she didn't work hard on control. I warned her many times, but she ignored me and grew bored with our lessons. She wanted to be me without the hard work."

Her grandmother touched the child's cheek and rubbed a smudge of chocolate from the top lip.

"You will be me someday. You will take my name and shine brighter than I in this city."

"Did you see this?" The man on her right once again interrupted her thoughts. He held out the magazine, showing her the newest sports car.

"I don't drive."

"You're kiddin'. I started driving when I was twelve. Could barely touch the pedals, but my dad believed a person wasn't too young for anything."

She wished she had stopped at the airport to buy a magazine or a book. Even if she didn't feel like reading, she could have at least pretended.

"Am I bothering you, miss?"

"Yes. I have a lot to think about before I get home."

"Sorry, just thought we could make the trip go faster if we chatted." He turned away from her and looked around for another seat, but could see none.

She wanted to ask him whether this was his first flight, but didn't want to start him talking again. Instead, she sank back into her thoughts.

The granddaughter knew she was a poor replacement for her grandmother. She feared the spirits, and knowing how her mother had died made her feel more uncomfortable. She couldn't open herself to the spirits and welcome them into her soul and heart. She feared losing control. But her grandmother persisted in teaching her, never allowing a day to go by without a lesson.

On dark nights when her grandmother would slide into a stupor, the spirit of Doctor John would visit. He'd tell her to go home, to steal away while she could. Her old wretched grandmother would return to the world on her own. The old woman didn't need a child waiting quietly for her.

"She would be disappointed in me."

"Nah, she may not even remember your being here. She's plotting out her vengeance with the spirits."

"Why aren't you advising her?"

"Because she doesn't trust me, child. She still thinks I want to usurp her."

"But you'd need a body for that."

"Hmmm. A young, healthy body." He would lean toward her, smelling of homemade hooch.

"Trying to scare me isn't going to make me go. Grandma warned me about you. She said, 'Doctor John will try to distract you, child. He will tease you and offer you his own powers, but he'll never share. He'll never reveal the potions that made him famous.' "

He looked over at Marie Laveau. "I remember when she was as young as you. The men would come to services to see her dance. Her body swayed and gyrated in perfect harmony to the music. But none of them got anything more than a look."

"Did you want more?"

"I'm a man and can still arouse myself by closing my eyes and seeing into the past. Her colorful dresses. Her lips defined in a deep red. Her skin wet from her efforts." He touched himself, but it didn't satisfy and his eyes opened and he glanced at Marie Laveau. "It sure isn't the same now. Some things must be taken in a split second or else they are gone forever."

Turbulence rocked the granddaughter into the present. She checked the time and decided to close her eyes and try for sleep.

Chapter Sixty-one

Some local youths polished a muscle car as loud music pounded out onto the street. Marie Laveau hated the sounds, and recalled when her appearance on the balcony would make everyone silent. She wouldn't waste her energy. She had to bring home her granddaughter and hold Liliana hostage for as long as she could. Perhaps her own granddaughter could take possession of Liliana. She would introduce them immediately on her granddaughter's return.

"Foolish old woman," she mumbled. "Thinking that he would love you again when he never had." Once she had spread her soft hands against Sade's flesh. Now her hands were bony and withered. In the past she would nibble and kiss his skin. Now the few teeth she had barely served to eat her porridge, and her lips were cracked and sore.

But this Liliana, even without a body, still held his love. Why?

"Grandma."

Marie Laveau smiled recognizing the voice of her granddaughter. She turned her head toward the doorway, and saw a frail young woman with dark circles under her eyes. The young woman held onto the door as if she would fall if she had to stand alone on her two feet.

"Has he been here yet?" she asked.

"Come over here, child. Sit at my feet so that I may see you up close."

The granddaughter walked carefully across the old cypress floor and sat on one of the throw rugs near the rocking chair.

Marie Laveau reached out to touch the granddaughter's hair, which felt like dried hay.

"What have you gone through? You have been hurt. I know he stole the gris-gris from you. Why did it take so long for you to come back?"

"He killed a woman in front of me, in my apartment. His rage scared me. I didn't know what to do." Teardrops flushed her cheeks. "I didn't expect anyone to die. I staked her with my own hands to prevent her from becoming a vampire. Very little blood came of that wound since he had already taken most of her blood. It could have been me he killed."

"No, no." Marie Laveau did not explain how she herself had urged him to kill. "Do you think I would have allowed that?"

"How could you have stopped him? You were so far away."

"Before you left I told you I would forever be with you." Marie Laveau wiped her granddaughter's tears away with her fingers.

Hope slipped softly around the granddaughter's shoulders and appeared to kiss her forehead with its forked tongue.

"Even Hope missed you, child. You've been very brave and I shall need you to be even braver."

"I've been weak. I froze when Sade killed the prostitute. I didn't do anything but sit and watch."

"That's all you were meant to do."

"What do you mean, Grandma?"

"Through that death I gained a bit more power over the vampire. Each of his killings enriches me. He no longer just feeds himself with these dead bodies. He also feeds my power."

"I don't want to take part in any more killings. Will you allow him to go away or will you kill him?"

"Sade is already dead. No one can kill him, but someone can destroy his body and send him off to the limbo he deserves."

"Is that what you plan to do?"

"I want him alive. Even after I'm gone I want him to exist and suffer for the great love he can't disown."

"Who does he love?"

"He has a daughter. A girl he made into a vampire and in turn vampires killed her in a cemetery. I've brought father and daughter together. Now I will sever those ties."

"Liliana. She is not his niece?"

"No, she is his bastard child by his wife's sister. A daughter of sin, my dear."

"Do they both know?"

"He has always known, but for Liliana this is new knowledge. You would think that she would hate him. Instead, she wants to see him, talk to him, forgive him, I'm sure."

"But should Liliana suffer for what her father did? She

has suffered for so long. Is there a way of releasing her and destroying him?"

Hope looped her body around the granddaughter's throat like a scarf.

"He suffers when Liliana suffers. If I free her, he will not care what I do to him." Marie Laveau leaned back and rocked herself. "I have very important work for you. You must prepare yourself to carry on when I am gone."

"You mean continue the vengeance."

"How will I be able to sleep if you don't? Tonight you will meet Liliana. Poor girl is filled with confusion and you want to keep her that way. Imagine what it must be like to have a father such as Sade."

"I have none, Grandmother."

"Your mother wanted a child, not a husband."

"And I wanted a father."

"You and Liliana can match stories, but never allow her to know your full feeling of loss. She could turn your own pain against you."

"I don't want to trap Liliana inside me."

Marie Laveau looked at her granddaughter's defiant face. The first time she had ever encountered this face on her child.

"You don't have to imprison her inside your own soul or body. No, you only must control her so that she can't escape your powers."

"But how powerful am I?"

"You are from my bloodline. Many generations removed from me, but still my blood circulates inside your body. You call me Grandmother, but we both know 'great' could be placed before that title many times over. Yet we have cast aside all the in-between Marie Laveaus so that we can touch each other's souls. I no longer exist. Grandmother is gone. You are Marie Laveau. Cater to me as you would to a deceased relative. Light candles on your altar for me. And when I truly die, wash my body with your hands. Lay me out in this room. Sit with me until my soul has found its home, then take gasoline, spread it over my body, and burn this house down. You see my Hope knows already that I'm gone. She caresses you." Marie Laveau reached out to touch the snake and it hissed at her. "She knows my time is gone. I've done what I could to twist my revenge from a false lover. He didn't even pity me, child."

"You would never want his pity."

"I thought not until I knew he wouldn't. A secret." Marie Laveau leaned forward and beckoned her granddaughter nearer. "I experienced no satisfaction when he stood before me. All the days and nights I had spent with him came back to me. And they were beautiful."

"Grandmother . . ."

Marie Laveau placed a finger on her granddaughter's lips.

"Shhh . . . and then I realized that I did carry his child. The child he will always love more than anyone. She may not have grown in my body, but I have her forever. You as the new Marie Laveau will carry his child too." She smiled contentedly until she saw the look on her granddaughter's face.

"Come, child. Let me heal your wound. You must have all your strength."

Repulsion soured the child's features, but she didn't deny her grandmother's request.

Chapter Sixty-two

The young woman looked into the mirror and did not see Marie Laveau. She saw clear skin without any of the lines and wrinkles that shattered her grandmother's face. Her hair was still dark, without the occasional bald spots. Her eyelids didn't look weak and heavy. Her lips were still worth kissing. Her brows still had the natural rich reddish-brown color.

Why must she give that up to become her grandmother sitting for hours with the spirits, pleading with them for favors or wrestling with them for power?

Generation after generation, Marie Laveau guided a chosen child into being her. Into walking the streets with her confident gait, her haunty self-reliance in every word she spoke, and the flash of magic that kept the followers quiet.

"I am Marie Laveau," she whispered, but the words didn't suit her voice. "Marie Laveau." She couldn't even remember her real name. She had been someone else before her mother died and left her with "Marie Laveau."

Louis Sade made love to Marie Laveau. No one had ever made love to the face in the mirror. Always in an embrace she would be Marie Laveau, because that way she could control the sexual magic. Use the sexual union for Marie Laveau's purposes.

When any man touched her, she offered it up to Marie Laveau. The old woman came to her and replaced the young woman's consciousness with her own. The old woman experienced the orgasms even as dried out as she was.

What had her own name been? The old woman had taken the birth certificate and burned it to ash in offering to one of the *loas*.

"Now you are me," the old woman said as the smoke cleared from the little cauldron.

"I am Marie Laveau."

Why am I not happy? Has the old woman ever experienced true happiness, or has she spent her life making note of all who did her wrong? Have any of her progeny ever been able to fill her seat of power as Vodou Queen?

The snake slid up the bathroom pipes to reach the young woman. It coyly peeked into the mirror.

"And what do you see, Hope?"

The snake opened wide its mouth and hit the mirror with its tongue. When it turned to face the young woman, it bobbed its head and moved forward as if about to strike. But it never touched the young woman, for it gave only a warning before dropping back onto the bathroom tile.

The granddaughter wondered whether the old woman

could possess this snake. Always open, the eyes of the snake followed the granddaughter's movements. It embraced her when she felt scared. It even smelled stale like the old woman.

She walked into the living room and immediately met the eyes of the old woman. The crinkle of the old woman's smile never made it to her eyes.

"I have named you and Hope has adopted you, child. Here is your family before you. It is a duty you must take up."

"How did you become Marie Laveau?"

"I have always been Marie Laveau, child."

"No, you were born a nameless baby. You suckled at someone's breast and your father . . . I know nothing of your parents."

"I am African, Native American, and European. My father was a wealthy white planter. My mother gave him pleasure in exchange for money. When her belly began to swell, he sent her away. Being a generous woman, my mother quickly became poor."

"What was your mother's name?"

"Edna, Naomi, who can remember?"

"You remember everything. Was her name Marie Laveau?"

"What are you asking?"

"Are you just one of the many Marie Laveaus?"

"I have told you stories about long ago."

"That's all they may be. Stories handed down from one Marie Laveau to the next. I'm the last."

"Nonsense, someday you'll meet a man. . . ."

"I cannot have children. While in Paris I was raped by

a stranger. He cut me deeply with a knife. The doctors told me that I was left unable to bear children. Unable to bear the next Marie Laveau."

The old woman stopped rocking. For a few minutes she seemed to be digesting what she had been told.

"Sade . . ."

"I told you the rapist was a stranger. A man who offered to help me on the street. I had just watched Sade kill the prostitute. Confused and vulnerable, I took his help."

"I can't die," the old woman said. "Marie Laveau must never die."

"You really are my grandmother. The original Marie Laveau is long dead. The vodou secrets, the hate, the history have been handed down generation after generation."

"And the power. Don't forget the power. Always there is one child to sit at Marie Laveau's feet and learn. I think Marie Laveau's thoughts. I remember the vampire's touch. His rejection. I can describe the rooms we lived in."

"Well-memorized stories. I bet you never think about the young woman you were. You believe Sade bedded you. You believe you've survived centuries.

"In the bathroom I stared into the mirror and couldn't remember my real name. You've cast a spell making who I was nonexistent. Don't you wish you could be someone else? Someone you were meant to be?"

"The spell is cast when the child is an infant. Your mother didn't want to give you up. That is why she wanted to be greater than me. She wanted to be able to fight my magic."

"She didn't die of a weak heart. She died fighting you in a trance."

"I entered her mind and challenged her. I took her heart into my hands and squashed it."

Gripped together tightly, the old woman's hands turned pale.

"Blood flowed in between my fingers. Real blood. Yes, your mother died in Haiti, but I reached out from this house and pulled her heart back to New Orleans." Exhausted, the old woman dropped her hands into her lap.

"Why couldn't you help me when I was in Paris?"

"Stupid child, the gris-gris that you lost to Sade would have bound us. Your mother and I always remained connected." The old woman smiled. "She carried the gris-gris I gave her next to her heart."

The granddaughter's hand instinctively reached for her chest.

Ah! Up then from the ground sprang I
And hailed the earth with such a cry
As is not heard save from a man
Who has been dead, and lives again.
About the tree my arms I wound;
Like one gone mad I hugged the ground;
I raised my quivering arms on high;
I laughed and laughed into the sky. . . .

—"Renascence"
Edna St. Vincent Millay

Chapter Sixty-three

I want back into the world again, Liliana declared. I want to see my father, touch him, act like a child again. These fevered thoughts exhilarated Liliana out of a too-long rest.

The old woman's heart beat, her blood spun through the body, and her breath gave life to them both. Liliana wanted the body. She would fight to gain control. The old woman talked way too much and had too much belief in her powers. Sade's enemy, still mortal, walked a dangerous path when she wielded her power in the spirit world.

"You have lived, now it is time for you to die," said Liliana. "You can hear me. Are you afraid to speak to me? You say you will never let me go free. I say I want your body. Die, old woman, and I will gladly take this wretched body as my own. I have a father to see and speak with now. I have a grandmother who is in need of taming.

"So silent. For once you are quiet. Do you fear me? Do you fear what I will do to grab your body?"

"You have no idea, Liliana, how to use the magic on your behalf. A vampire isn't magic. You're a demon risen from hell and will never see the Lord's face," stated the old woman.

"I may not see my spiritual father, but I have a father made of flesh and blood. I'll not give him up.

"You will die. Death is closer than you can imagine. The older you get, the closer death comes, and the more vulnerable you become."

"You want my aches and pains. You want my faltering step. My tired eyes that can barely see. None of this will belong to you. I know my death. It waits here with me. I'll breathe death in when all is complete."

"You speak of death as if it were your friend, crazy old woman."

"You know what it's like to be near to death. You carry death with you when you feed."

"Never!"

"Can you say you have never killed in the mad fury of your hunger?" A few seconds of silence. "Suddenly you are the one to remain silent. I have courted death and made concessions to it. It has agreed to wait for me."

"Death cannot touch me anymore, old woman. But even I will admit that death can still make demands on my soul. Sometimes I have stolen away lives for death, but I never embraced death the way you have. Death is a fake friend, old woman. It laughs at you and will have its way when it is ready."

Chapter Sixty-four

Marie Laveau forced herself to her feet and called for her granddaughter. Marie Laveau had been dozing and didn't know whether the child had left the house. She managed to move her weak body from room to room hoping to find the child. She had to move her plan forward now for she didn't trust this Liliana. At first Liliana seemed so compliant, so manageable, until she learned the identity of her father.

The front door slammed and Marie Laveau relaxed, returning to her rocking chair.

"I worried that you were gone, child."

"No, I'm back. You can't easily get rid of me. Matter of fact no one can."

Sade's mother-in-law stood in the doorway. Dressed in leather and carrying a black lace fan, she looked every bit the dominatrix. The boots stretched up her legs and barely touched her knees. The heels had to be at least six inches high.

"Why are you back?" Marie Laveau pulled her shawl from the table and wrapped it around her shoulders.

"I want Liliana set free."

Marie Laveau watched the woman strut into the room.

"Please come no closer. The stench of your perfume makes it hard for me to breathe."

"Certainly smells better than the decay you have hidden under all those rags."

"Did Sade send you?"

"No, he's intent on finding your granddaughter. Seems he wants to tear her throat out."

"And you come here to threaten me with that?"

"You don't want to see anything happen to your granddaughter. You sent her off for a bit of a dalliance with Louis, but you probably figured she needed some fun."

"My granddaughter doesn't need, want, or deserve Sade."

"I've heard he's really good. But you could tell me about that." The mother-in-law dusted off the love seat and sat. "I'm willing to listen if you're willing to tell."

"Get out of my house, you cheap whore."

"Not cheap. But I do have a heart of gold. That's why I'm here. You see, Sade will kill your granddaughter. He won't make her into a vampire if that's what you're hoping for. No, he's decided to kill her. However, if you were to free Liliana, he may be made to change his mind."

"I doubt he listens to much you say."

"Allow Sade and Liliana to say good-bye."

"He still wouldn't believe I had set her free. What would stop me from calling her back?"

"The fact that your granddaughter will end up dead."

"She's strong. She can . . ."

"Overcome a vampire, especially a powerful, cruel

vampire? Invite him here and convince him. Convince both of us that Liliana is free."

"If he kills my granddaughter, he will never see or hear from Liliana again. I'll send her deep into the spirit world with the hags and demons."

"I've been there. It's empty. A vacuum. No ogres flitting around or gremlins with pointy ears. You see, Sade destroyed my body and I wandered through that terrible fog until I found my opening back into the world."

"You took another's body?"

"She wasn't using it and as you can see it was in good shape. Only problem was that she was staked, but I managed to get help with that." The mother-in-law smiled proudly.

"You hope Liliana will find her way back?"

"Sade doesn't want her back in any shape or form, and I fear she might come back as you."

"You're willing to have her continue in that fog you described?"

The other woman nodded.

"But how can I make Sade believe me?"

"Bat your eyes at him and give him a bit of hip-swivel. On second thought, best to look vulnerable and sincere."

"I'm an old woman near death and don't want to continue this vendetta against Sade. I want my granddaughter to live in peace. I will free Liliana. I swear on my soul that I will free his daughter. I'll send her to him one last time, then I will destroy the vévé."

"The vévé?"

"I use flour and ash to draw the symbolic designs that call Liliana to me. I will draw the designs on paper and burn them in a cauldron of charcoal. You may even watch."

"Doesn't matter if I watch or not. I wouldn't know one vévé from another. However, if we find out you haven't freed Liliana, then both you and your granddaughter are dead. There's one of you for each of us. I think I'll leave you for Louis. I'm sure your blood would be too randy for me."

The mother-in-law stood.

"I'll tell Louis about your offer. He'll let your granddaughter live, although I'm not too sure about you."

Chapter Sixty-five

"Ah, Marie, what kind of fool are you?"

"Excuse me, Louis?"

Sade shook his head and walked to the window. "Do you believe Marie Laveau?"

"Of course not, but she can be forced into freeing Liliana. I told her that both she and her granddaughter would be killed if she didn't free our Liliana."

"And how will she get her revenge on me?"

"I don't know. She could stake you or cast some hoodoo spell on you. It doesn't matter as long as Liliana is free. Think about it, Sade. You kill her granddaughter, then what? She'll never give up Liliana. This vendetta will go on until the end of time. Why don't you take a nap, talk it over with Liliana, and then make a decision?"

"You speak of my dreams as if they were personal conferences."

"Yeah. Listen, don't you want to know how Liliana feels about you now that she knows the truth? Be brave.

Confront the girl. You and she have always had a decent relationship, certainly not perfect. She may be thrilled to have a father. I'll even stay and wait for you to wake."

"That gives me no solace, Marie."

Sade looked out the window and watched a drunk stagger down the street. People coming from the opposite direction attempted to avoid him, but instead got into each other's way. New Orleans tired Sade.

"What should I say to Liliana?" Sade asked.

"Talk about how she feels. Most importantly, make sure she doesn't seek to gain power over the crone's body. That, I believe, is our most important objective."

"What do I say? The gray nothingness in which you exist is far better than being an old woman? Just ask your grandmother?" Sade turned toward Marie.

"You have a marvelous sense of humor, Louis. Someday I hope to be able to enjoy it."

Sade closed the window and drew the curtains. He turned and walked toward the door in the spare bedroom. When he opened the door, the coffin stood with the lid opened waiting for him.

"Marie, it would be far easier for me to take revenge. Rip out that young woman's throat and leave her body on Marie Laveau's doorstep. Let the old woman keep Liliana until the day she dies, and then Liliana will be free forever."

"You'll never be able to rest until Marie Laveau is gone."

"Then perhaps I should rip out *her* throat."

Marie moved closer to Sade, but made sure she stayed outside his reach.

"You're afraid of Marie Laveau. You're unsure of how strong her power is. She might be able to burden you with greater hexes than what she has already done. She may be able to torture Liliana. She may be able to destroy all of us."

"What is Liliana's world like? You were there for a brief time. Describe what she is experiencing to me."

"It's similar to walking around on a foggy day. Only there's an absence of sound. You think you may hear something, but can never be sure. I found myself thinking that I'd never hear another sound, not a word. Music couldn't . . ."

"Soothe you. The way music soothes the rest of the world's beasts."

Marie smiled, moved closer to Sade, and reached out to touch his shoulder.

"No, Louis. Music couldn't make me happy. You know I like to sing and dance." She stopped and thought a while. "A man could never give me pleasure and I would be wasting all my talents. Artwork and books didn't exist. Unruly children couldn't annoy me. Tempting smells no longer tempted. Never again the taste of blood. Oh, how thirsty I was, Louis. I had no tongue, but still felt parched. I missed drinking the most. I didn't need the blood, but I craved it more than ever. I thought I had spent days screaming, but there is no time there. There was only one object I could center on besides your feet." She smirked at him. "My skull. You kept my skull at the foot of your coffin. That realization made me believe in myself and understand that the world still existed and I could return somehow. I believe Liliana has centered on you, Louis, her father. All this time she thought everything had finished. She desired nothing and no one wanted her. She loves you, Louis."

"She can never come back as Liliana."

"Am I still your mother-in-law?"

Sade turned and looked at Marie. "At the end of time, Marie, we will all be thirsty."

"I don't think about the end, Louis. Maybe it will never come. And if it does, what can we do about it? Rest, Louis, and say your good-bye. Liliana has a thirst for more than blood."

I know I might have lived in such a way
As to have suffered only pain:
Loving not man nor dog;
Not money even; feeling
Toothache perhaps, but never more than an hour away
From skill and novocaine;
Making no contacts, dealing with life through agents . . .

—From "Fontaine, Je Ne Boirai Pas De Ton Eau!"
Edna St. Vincent Millay

Chapter Sixty-six

The ballroom stood decorated with flowers of every kind and color. The walls were painted a soft peach. Black granite tiles covered the floors. Wisps of delicate lace hung at every window. Mythological murals spread across the ceiling. And illumination came from pastel candles set in golden candelabra.

A chord of music began as Sade walked into the room. The doors behind Sade closed, revealing the intricate details of gold gilt designs.

A single round table covered with silken linens waited in the middle of the room. Two intricately carved dining chairs had been placed at the table. True silverware studded the top of the table, and slim champagne glasses with ruby stems and round flat bottoms waited to be filled. White-on-white bone china reflected the candles' glow.

"Liliana," Sade called.

Doilylike place cards etched in gold attracted his attention. He picked them up to read.

"The Marquis de Sade," said one. The other simply read, "His Daughter."

He flung them back onto the table and thought about exiting when he noticed an opened set of double doors leading to a garden. A full moon lit the garden, and he saw the shadow of a woman on the red brick patio.

On his way to the opened double doors, his hands felt empty. He thought of the gifts he would bring her as a child, as a teen, and the small animals he would bring her for meals when she was a vampire. Small cuddly animals that she would take in as pets instead of as rations.

Flowers, he thought, looking around the room. He spied a turquoise vase overflowing with white roses sprinkled with thin webs of greenery. He piled the white roses into his arms and continued out to the patio.

A deep red coral dress hugged Liliana's body and barely touched the floor.

"Liliana."

She turned away from looking at the moon and faced Sade.

"These roses are the best I can do, but they don't compare to your stunning beauty and innocence." He spoke the word "innocence" softly, fearing she would rebuke him for taking that very gift from her.

"Father," she said, running to him. "They are beautiful and every one is perfect." She fondled the petals with joy.

"I believe I can find a vase for them if you come inside."

She giggled and daintily stepped over the threshold. Immediately she saw the turquoise vase and offered it to Sade.

"May I keep one with me?" she asked.

"Of course," he said, replacing the vase on its stand.

"Have you prepared supper for us?" she asked, seating herself at the dining table.

Sade laughed nervously. "I think the table is merely set for ambience," he said, taking the seat across from her.

A broad smile lighted her face and her hands never remained still.

"I feel like this is a birthday celebration," she said. "How old would I be? I've lost all track of time. I don't even know what month or year this is."

Sade ached for his daughter. He took her hands in his and kissed each slender finger. He noticed that her nails were short but finely filed to perfection. He caught sight of his ring, and remembered how he had taken it back from her hand. His mouth soured and he dropped her hands.

"You forgive me, Liliana?"

"I'm delighted to finally know the truth. I realize Grandmother would never have allowed you or my mother to admit . . ." Shyly she looked down at the table.

"We always were proud of you."

"From a distance. I'm sorry. I don't want to ruin this moment by being a sulky child. Not when this is all so new."

"Are you lonely, Liliana?"

"Not anymore. I shall always have you."

"This is still only a dream for us, Liliana. There is an old woman hovering about us and she is making this possible. But she can also take all this away from us and will."

"But I can defeat her, Father. I love saying 'Father.' I never could before."

"This old woman hates me. She wants to punish me and used you to reach me. I believe an understanding has finally been worked out and this woman has agreed to set your soul free."

"Free? To do what?"

Sade's head pounded. He wouldn't be able to accept tears, not when she looked so lovely.

"The color of your dress enhances your skin tone," he said.

"You came to tell me something, but you're afraid what I will do or say. Do you still want me to go away? Are you refusing my love once again?"

If he stood and walked from the room, would Marie Laveau let him, or would she force him to stay and suffer his daughter's unhappiness?

"Should I call for champagne? Perhaps there's a waiter stashed among all these flowers. I find that my mouth is quite dry."

"From the lies you are about to tell?" she said.

"I won't lie to you, Liliana. That I won't do." Sade thought about reaching for her hands again, but feared the touch of her flesh might make him hesitate.

"You can't come back, Liliana. I don't want you back in my life. Love is too expensive and I refuse to pay the cost. I lost you several years ago." He looked at the ring on his finger and wondered whether there existed a way to give it to her. He slipped the ring from his finger. "Give me your hand." She reached across the table with her left hand softly touching his skin. He slid the ring onto her finger. He wanted so much for her to have it.

"I will come back to you, Father."

"Lord, whatever you do don't take over the body of that ancient hag who holds us here. You'd be infirm and ugly."

"You're supposed to think that I could never be ugly no matter how my physical condition changed. That's what a loving father would say."

"I'm not a very good father. Your half brothers and half sister would quickly inform you of that."

"But they're not here. You didn't choose to turn them into vampires because you didn't want them around forever. However, me you couldn't resist." She gave him a sly smile.

"No, you can't win me over. Our relationship ends here. I never will see you again. If you should attempt to come back, I will destroy you." He saw that her expression did not change. "Believe me, Liliana, there is no one I love more than myself. I will do what is best for me." He stood.

"Allow me to walk you to the door, Father."

He walked around the table to hug her. He felt the delicacy of her bones, the softness of her skin, the scent of female hormones, and the hotness of her breath.

"Stay put, Liliana. Don't walk with me or follow me. And never reach out to me again. If somehow you make it back into the world, don't ever seek me out because I will destroy you. I am finished with you." He pushed her back into her seat.

Chapter Sixty-seven

Mesmerized, Sade's mother-in-law watched his flesh flush red hot, so hot that she could smell the coffin's satin burn. Within a few seconds his flesh turned a frozen blue that chilled the entire room.

When he opened his eyes, she asked, "Are you free of her?"

"I can never be free of her. All I can do is ignore her and her memory. I told her I would destroy her if she ever returned and came to me."

"Would you?"

"The prime person in the world for me is me. Loving someone makes one vulnerable. Yes, I will destroy what I love."

"You've proved that over and over again, Louis. She should be able to believe you since you've destroyed her many times over." Marie turned away from the coffin and went back to the living room. "Does this mean you also love me?" She looked over her shoulder and coyly smiled.

He appeared in the doorway.

"I suppose I'm rash since I decimate whatever causes strong feelings in me whether they be good or bad. Certainly in your case what drove me was hate."

She walked over to him and tried to place her hands on his shoulders, but he gripped her wrists.

"Louis, we've been together long enough that you should be able to get over the differences that may have made your pre-vampire life miserable." She closed her eyes. "Hmmm, your hands are strong."

"That's why it was so easy for me to rip apart your old body."

Her eyes popped open and sincerity softened her expression. "I forgive you, Louis."

He let her go and pushed her out of his way.

"Now how will we know whether Marie Laveau will keep her part of the bargain?"

Marie shrugged. "Certainly, if you dream of Liliana again, we know she didn't. The problem that bothers me is whether she has freed Liliana's soul."

"I almost don't care," he said, dropping onto the leather sofa.

"What? You do care. You've always doted on Liliana, even when the ridiculous child wouldn't drink human blood."

"That's never been a problem for you. You suck whoever you can dry," he said.

"You mean that figuratively, I know. I'm careful not to kill my clients. They pay me a lot of money to shed their blood. Why should I pass up the opportunity?"

"I want this over and I want to be back in Paris by the end of the week," he said.

"Then you should visit the Vodou Queen tonight. Make peace with her. Maybe even apologize for Liliana's sake. We can't leave until we know it is truly finished and that Liliana is free again."

"Liliana may fight Marie Laveau."

"Does she so strongly want to return to this world?"

"Yes." Quickly he looked down at his hand. The ring remained on his finger. "I tried to give her this ring. Obviously I couldn't pass anything to her in a dream. But stupidly I tried. I'm sorry I made the gesture. Liliana may misread the situation and think that I really do want her back."

"Do you, Louis?"

"I told you. . . ."

"Yes, Louis, I heard you. But now I'm asking you to look deep inside yourself. Do you want her back? Would you accept her no matter what she looked like? And think, don't rush to give me an answer. Don't even bother to give me an answer right now. Think about her coming back and how you would feel."

Chapter Sixty-eight

The granddaughter walked the streets of Old New Orleans slowly. The houses and restaurants looked the same. The seedy joints still added lively color to the dark streets. On Bourbon Street the store that sold only condoms did an excellent business offering multicolors and fun shapes. And the strip place across the street had black and white photographs of the latest live sex acts plastered across its windows.

She kept arguing with herself about whether or not she should return to her grandmother. To her real grandmother, she reminded herself.

Eventually, she found herself in front of the cemetery in which the real Marie Laveau rested. No one else walked these streets at this hour, and only an occasional car drove by. She had heard stories about the city's ruffians who stalked the cemeteries hoping to prey on unaware tourists, but at this hour there wouldn't be any point to that behavior.

The gate appeared to be locked, but on closer examination she noticed that the padlock hadn't been closed completely. Carefully, she undid the padlock and opened the squeaky gate. In the stillness of the late night, the noise sounded loud and scratchy.

As she walked into the cemetery, she smelled the remains of incense. It was too dark to see, and she kept walking blindly on the familiar path. Marie Laveau's mausoleum had flowers, most nearly dead, and several combs and brushes laid out on the ground. She smiled, remembering that her ancestor had been a hairdresser to some of the wealthiest families in New Orleans giving her access to up-to-date gossip. As she moved, her right foot kicked several pennies that had been left as offerings.

The granddaughter knelt and started to tidy the makeshift altar, setting aside the rotted remains of flowers and adding a few pennies of her own.

"Mamma Laveau, what should I do? Did you mean for your life to be extended through these two centuries? Each generation one of your progeny has given up her life to be you. Must I follow all the others?"

She thought she smelled perfume filling the air. Perfume or maybe hair conditioner or one of the many herbs Marie Laveau had used in her business. A sign that she listened?

"Have these centuries been spent seeking final vengeance on one of your past lovers? Is he that important? I no longer know my own name. Only your name passes my lips when I am asked."

The granddaughter's knees hurt, and she repositioned herself into a seated position. The night air felt soothing after the long hot day, and the silence gave some relief from the urgency of her problem.

"My grandmother doesn't have much time left. She'll not have a mausoleum as you do. Already she has told me that her body is to be burned and her ashes laid at your feet as if she had never existed. Is that to be my future? I cannot bear children, so I will never have to sacrifice a child to you. The vendetta is at an end. Sade is here in New Orleans and his Liliana is being held captive by my grandmother. What are we to do with them? Shall I bring you his staked heart? Or is having him exist in misery without his Liliana preferable?"

She looked straight ahead at the mausoleum and thought she saw the reflection of her own face. Her face or Marie Laveau's face? She touched her head and felt no tignon, but the reflection wore a dark-colored tignon.

"Mamma Laveau." Reaching her hand out, she felt the cool stone of the mausoleum. "I'm sorry I will be the first to fail you, but all the hate and sorrow and denial has to end with me. I can offer up my life to you, but I will never outlive your lover, Sade. Forgive me, Mamma Laveau. But must I waste my own life in this centuries-old pursuit?"

The vision before her eyes wavered, changing into a long, slender viper, its tongue reaching toward her. A hiss sounded behind her, and she turned to see a snake twisting and turning in the process of shedding its skin. When it finished, the head rose up and struck out at the granddaughter. She felt a sharp pain on her forearm, and when she looked she found a red mark. The snake slithered away leaving the shed skin behind.

The granddaughter picked up the skin, remembering that her grandmother had used Hope's shed skin to make the potion that gave her long life.

She turned back to the mausoleum to see a smiling

Marie Laveau staring back at her. Looking down at her own arm, the granddaughter saw the wound on her arm fade as she watched.

"You want me to use this snake skin the way all the other progeny have."

The smile on the vision's face grew broader, and tears flowed quickly down the granddaughter's cheeks.

Chapter Sixty-nine

Sade's mother-in-law left him to ponder the question she had asked. Did he really not want Liliana to return? What would he truly do if Liliana managed to return to this world?

The stairs leading down to the street creaked, and the faded, threadbare carpet covering the steps did little to cushion the noise. On the first floor, she could hear the rowdy bar with its lurid music and drunken catcalls.

"Pathetic beasts," she murmured to herself as she opened the door leading out onto the sidewalk. "Old men taking advantage of young girls trying to make a living."

An elderly man passing by with his wife heard her comment and, startled, looked directly into her eyes. Marie stuck out her tongue and flashed him a breast. The man's wife pulled him along while he flushed a bright red.

Marie ended up down by the water. Tourists were

strolling, and hawkers offered their services as guides through the "scary" streets of New Orleans.

One group had dressed for their jobs with capes, black clothes, and heavy makeup. One interesting guide wore a top hat and seemed to be missing his front teeth. Not to worry, though, he still had his fangs. Not a very good set, she thought, but how much could this actor make on the streets?

"We have a special tonight. Our Lady Elvira is handing out five-dollar coupons. Yes, instead of fifteen dollars, tonight you may see the hidden parts of Old New Orleans for only ten dollars."

With nothing else to do and out of curiosity, Marie grabbed a coupon and paid her ten dollars. She wanted to see how the vampires of New Orleans lived.

The man with the top hat and missing teeth called the first fifteen tourists up the stairs to be closer to the water and away from the constant babble of his associate. Marie followed the man with the top hat, missing teeth, and mourning coat.

"Now I want you all to stay close together. Don't want to be searching for missing bodies at the end of the tour." He passed through the group, collecting the tickets with rough hands that had long fingernails painted black. She thought she caught the whiff of alcohol, and decided she definitely had when she saw his bloodshot eyes.

"Does anyone mind if I smoke?" He already had the pack of cigarettes in his shaky hands. No one dared to deny this man his fix. "Tonight I'll have an assistant." He pointed toward a bland fellow who stood about ten feet away. He didn't seem to want to be connected to his coworker. "Yes, he will make sure there are no stragglers and watch for traffic when we walk the side streets." His eye makeup bled slightly onto his face.

"How long is the tour?" asked one of the party.

"Two hours. But halfway through we'll be taking a break for something to drink and to use the rest room."

The group reacted as if this was fair enough.

"You will hear many strange tales. Stories that will curdle your blood." He turned away for a few moments to cough. When he turned back, he quickly took another puff on his cigarette. She saw nicotine stains that would probably never be washed off his fingers.

The guide led the group forward and passed on the tickets to the man still hawking the tours.

Marie wondered whether this would be worthwhile. Would she gain anything after two hours of listening to this charlatan? She looked the group over, and decided she might be able to obtain a nice meal.

"Keep walking. Watch for the cars," said the guide, who started talking to two lovely girls not more than nineteen years old.

The group had spread out, with half the people on the sidewalk and the other half walking out in the center of the street, making perfect targets for drunken drivers.

Suddenly a bicyclist in a flowing red-lined black cape started corralling the tourists.

"Hey, Nick and Igor, make sure they stay on the sidewalk." The cape brushed against her arm, and she squinted in disgust at the one-hundred-percent polyester.

Squished together on the sidewalk, the group slowed its pace to baby steps. Finally Igor, the guide, called everyone around him.

"In the late seventeen hundreds the gray house across the street was flooded with blood. The man who lived there . . ."

Two little boys pushed their way up close to the guide and stared at the house with open mouths.

Tender little morsels, she thought. But not enough blood in them for a decent meal. Several of the plump tourists caught her eye. One man wore Bermuda shorts with a Hawaiian shirt. His belly pushed out the surfboards decorating the material. The woman with him weighed at least half as much as he did. Her knobby knees and bleached red hair gave her a fragile look. She looked like a runner. What did the two of them have in common? Marie wondered.

"Don't dawdle. This way," Igor called, forging ahead.

Of course, she said to herself, he wears the top hat so we can see him.

"Behind this wall is a convent. The sisters who live here are cloistered. They never speak to anyone or come out onto the streets of New Orleans. During the day there is nothing but silence here, but at night people have claimed to hear the wailing of victims that feed the vampire sisters."

The gates of the convent opened and a car pulled out driven by a young man. He stopped when he saw the tour group and yelled out at the guide.

"Igor, the sisters want to speak with you."

A flummoxed Igor merely smiled guiltily and waved at the driver.

After this encounter, the guide decided to take a break at one of the bars on the side street, but the group had to wait since the previous tour group hadn't left yet.

"Just a few minutes and we can stop here. The rest rooms are in the rear just under the Bud sign."

"Hey, Igor!"

Standing on a balcony over the bar were a pair of guys who could have applied for Igor's job. Then again, Marie thought, maybe they had his job but were on break.

"You've got the best guide in this city," yelled one of the men.

"Thanks, Stu," he called back.

"It's true. I see them come along here all the time so I know." The man raised his bottle of beer in salute to the guide.

"We can go in now. The bar is emptying out," said Igor.

A man in a red devil suit held up his pitchfork in case his tour group couldn't recognize him.

Inside the bar, most of the tourists formed a line for the unisex rest room. The rest ordered cold drinks.

"How do you like the tour so far?" Igor asked her. Marie hadn't seen him sneaking up, and her body gave a slight jolt of surprise.

"Wonderful, Igor."

"I noticed you are alone and wanted to make sure you're not too frightened. Last half of the tour gets a little bloody, but if you need someone to take you home, I'll gladly accommodate."

She wished he would put the bottle of beer down; enough booze tainted his blood. She slid her rear onto a stool and let her tight black leather skirt ride up her thighs revealing more of her fishnet stockings. He didn't miss the view.

"I may be able to give you some more scary stories to tell," she said, passing the palm of her right hand across his cheek.

"Always can use more material." He smiled, and the gap in his teeth made her wonder whether "easy" would be a good reason to drain this man.

Several tourists crowded around Igor with questions. He chuckled and fed them some more of his pap.

"Time to go. Another group wants to come in," said Igor. A group of tourists peeked through the window standing behind their bloody Frankenstein.

Back on the street, Igor announced that he had something to show the group. He claimed his blood clotted quickly and he didn't have to worry about injuries.

"Okay, watch this closely. Can everyone see? But don't step out in front of a car." After all, it was only he who could heal within moments.

He dug his black nails into his forearm and red blood gushed from his flesh. The tourists in front stepped farther back, and the tourists in back craned to see what would happen next.

The eyes of the two nine-year-old boys in the group popped open. One said to the other, "Man, that's so cool."

The other boy agreed enthusiastically, and the first boy whispered to his friend, "I can't wait to grow my fingernails long."

Marie shook her head and sniffed at the red goop running down Igor's arm.

"In the meantime," Igor said, using a tissue to sop up the mess, "let me tell you . . ."

Later she'd show him what his blood really looked like.

"I can't seem to stop the bleeding," Igor yelled to his assistant. "I need more bandages."

The assistant slowly meandered over to Igor while a couple of the tourists offered to take him to the hospital.

"No, no. It's all right, it will eventually stop bleeding," he reassured them.

By the time they had passed the house with the corncob fence, the bleeding had ended. A convenient happening since the tour was over.

His assistant passed out Igor's card. Seems he was available for parties and suppers, although Marie couldn't think of any mortal who would invite him to dinner. However, she'd have him for dinner.

She waited impatiently while the tourists thanked him and moved on. The two nineteen-year-old girls stood close to him admiring how quickly his flesh had healed.

"I don't even see a scar. Do you, Suz? That's absolutely amazing. You really do heal quickly."

The miniskirted brats didn't want to move on. Mesmerized by his healing prowess, they moved closer for a better view. Igor had no problem displaying himself. Marie figured he had lots more to display to these girls, but she didn't have time for that. She moved in front of him to remind him of his promise.

"Oh, ah . . ."

"Marie," she said.

"Yes. This is Suz and . . ." He turned expectantly to the other girl, but she remained engrossed in fingering the flesh on his forearm.

"Lola," said Suz.

"Why don't we head back to my place for a bite to eat."

The girls giggled and looked shyly at each other.

"I can show you more of this kind of stuff," he said, holding up his arm.

You bet you will, Marie thought.

Childhood is not from birth to a certain age and at a certain age
The child is grown, and puts away childish things.
Childhood is the kingdom where nobody dies.

—"Childhood Is the Kingdom Where Nobody Dies"
Edna St. Vincent Millay

Chapter Seventy

From an early age Liliana had understood that death loomed like a cloud over our heads. She had no father, and most acted as if he had died and left nothing but her to remember him by, yet even she did not know his identity. At three she found herself at her mother's grave watching relatives she had never seen before hug her grandmother. Most of the people present avoided the little girl, who couldn't quite understand why the big box held her mother. Wasn't the box uncomfortable? Could Mamma even hear the nice things said about her? She watched the box lowered into the ground. Grandma slipped a rose in her hand and walked her to the deep hole. Tense and scared, the girl gripped the rose tightly. Grandmother had to pry her tiny fingers from the stem, and she watched as the flower also disappeared inside the hole.

Uncle . . .

No, Father lifted her into the air and carried her away from the dark scene. And as he carried her back to the carriage, she wondered how Mamma would get out of the hole. Would someone scoop up the box? She looked over his shoulder and watched as each relative and friend walked away from the hole. No one bothered to stop and help Mamma out of the ground.

She remembered calling to her mother, and once again heard the panic in her own voice.

But now she couldn't even recall what Mother had looked like. Didn't know whether Mother had light or dark hair. Was she tall or short? Heavy or slender? And did her voice soothe Liliana when she lay in her cradle?

Her father carried a warm, light scent on his slender, medium-height frame. His strong hands tickled her belly and his voice assured her of safety.

She finally knew her father and all the memories attached to him. Why would she walk away from him now?

The woman who possessed her soul listened to her thoughts, she knew. The shadow of the woman's being pressed up against Liliana, wanting to know more of this love.

"He will always love me and resent you," Liliana said.

"But you are the cause of his deepest pain, my child. He doesn't want you back. He has told you so. Yet you hold on to a dream, an image of love, not real love. He would have me send you back into the void to live forever alone, untouched by any emotion. Is that what love is, Liliana?"

"Will you set me free?"

"What if I could make Sade's and your souls one? You could live inside his mind. Enjoy the perversities in which he participates. Learn how closed off he is to love."

"You didn't answer my question. Will you set me free?"

"I am old and cannot hold you inside myself for much

longer, but do you want to be set free to return to the void? I doubt it, not after feeling a hint of the world's adventures."

"I do not want to be one with my father. I want to be his daughter."

"You mean you don't want to share in your father's sins even though there is no possibility of salvation for you anyway?"

"He will always be my father. Let Grandmother and others rave about his behavior. I will remain still."

"You'll not encourage him on?" Marie Laveau asked.

"I only want him to be my father."

"And not your uncle? I foolishly thought his love for me would make him feel guilty, beg for my forgiveness. I was as great a fool as you are, Liliana.

"Go back to sleep, child. There is nothing left for you in this world. The emptiness and quiet of your world is preferable to the bleakness of mine. For many years I've let the distractions that abound in this world carry me through repetitious days of pain. Losses could always be expected, but I thought I had a goal. I've waited for this day, and now . . ."

"You gain no pleasure," Liliana whispered.

Chapter Seventy-one

The old woman felt a delicate veil fall into her hands. A familiar smell made her shiver and look down at her hands.

"Show me how to use that," the granddaughter said.

"But Hope wasn't due to . . ."

"The skin doesn't belong to Hope. I received it from the real Marie Laveau, at the foot of her grave."

"A sign," the old woman whispered. She smiled up at her granddaughter, but saw only a brooding frown in response. "Of course, I'll teach you everything and Hope will replenish your store when you need it."

"And what of the small rattler?"

The old woman gently handed the snake skin back and then lifted the terrarium in her hands. The rattler shivered and rattled its tail.

"This poison is meant for me to use at the proper time." She dragged her finger across the glass, and the rattler struck out at her, hitting the glass so rapidly and hard that the old woman almost dropped the container. She laughed and settled the terrarium back on the table.

"There is a vévé you must learn to draw."

"And what spirit will the vévé call?" asked the granddaughter.

This younger Marie Laveau does not know how to bend and reshape herself. "Brittle," the old woman cursed under her breath. "You shouldn't ask questions so much."

"I must be able to protect myself from whatever I call."

The old woman nodded her head. "But don't resist the spirits. Let them come freely into your body and work with them for your own causes."

"For Marie Laveau's causes."

"You are Marie Laveau."

"No, I'm trapped. If I walk away, you'll reach out for my heart as you did with my mother."

"Foolish, insipid girl. We are all born with a purpose. Serve yours without complaining."

"Do I exist only to punish a vampire?"

The crone sighed. "There is charity work for you to do. You have watched me visiting homes belonging to the poor and ill. Through you the spirits can take away the blights that leaden their souls with sickness. I've already showed you the wonders of many herbs and animals. Why, a warmed poultice of mashed beetles can draw out the bad humors that make one's lungs feel heavy. You remember the hideous sores on that babe a few months ago. The mother's sleeves dripped with the leaking pus. And we took that child into our arms and sprinkled the child with graveyard dust calling upon Gede to regenerate the child. And by the time the black and violet candles burned down, the babe's flesh had mostly healed. Slowly the baby regained its strength, and now wails strongly with his demands."

The granddaughter knelt down in front of the crone, resting her hands containing the snake skin on the crone's lap.

"I want to heal. Teach me all you know so that I may assist in the birth of babies, calm childhood fevers, take pain from the maimed, and comfort the unhappy. Let me aid in bringing peace to the dying and consolation to those they leave behind. I would do all those things without a single complaint. But don't soil me with your vengeance. Allow God to punish Sade and Liliana, and in Marie Laveau's name I will do good vodou magic."

"Punishing evil is part of doing good, child. Sade must pay for not only leaving our ancestor, but also for the many lives he has touched with his blackened hands. He must suffer for every sin he's committed."

"Let me destroy him then. I will keep him from harming others."

The crone rose up, kicking her granddaughter away from her feet. "That won't satisfy Marie Laveau. He must pay over and over again."

"And so must Liliana?"

"She's a thorn he'll never be able to pluck. She'll make him bleed for eternity."

"Let him fester in his own guilt."

"No! He must be reminded constantly of what he has created and thrown away."

"Must I accept your anger as well as your magic?" the

granddaughter asked, looking up from where she lay on the floor.

The crone found herself panting and the more she fought for air, the more her lungs seized until darkness fell upon her.

Chapter Seventy-two

The granddaughter crawled toward the still old woman lying on the floor. She reached out gingerly to settle her hand on the old woman's chest. She dared not add pressure, but did test for movement. A slow, unsteady rise and fall told her that her grandmother still lived. Kneeling she took an old shriveled hand in hers and tried to lend some of her own warmth to the flesh.

"Grandmother," she whispered, leaning close to the crone's ear. "I love you."

The old woman's face twitched slightly, perhaps in pain, whether physical or mental the granddaughter could not know. The lips had turned a shade of purple and quivered as if trying to find words.

"I love you," the granddaughter repeated, hoping the words would give comfort and hold the ancient soul to the earth. "Don't die yet. You've not completed your work. I am here to learn from you." She noted that the old woman's breath had become more regular.

After settling her grandmother's hand back onto the floor, the granddaughter stood. She squatted briefly in order to scoop up the ancient body. The mass of rags weighed hardly anything, and she had to clutch the figure tightly to feel the frail, slender, hollow bones beneath.

Moving slowly, she walked to the door of the bedroom and crossed the threshold. The bed, still unmade, beckoned her forward. She placed her grandmother on the lace-trimmed sheets, gathering the blanket from the bottom of the bed to spread across the still form. She caught sight of the altar at the foot of the bed. The flames of several gold and black candles flickered. The Blessed Mother had her head bowed in sorrow, while several smaller statues of saints seemed to stare across the expanse at the old woman. The granddaughter made the sign of the cross and knelt before the altar.

"Mother Mary, give my grandmother peace. She has carried a great burden for too many years. Let her slip free from the tethers that have tied her to this house for so many years. She once had a name different from the one she carried for so many years. Help her to remember and regain the independence that name offers. Let her die not as a shadow of one long dead, but as a true child of your Son."

The granddaughter returned to the old woman and sat on the bed. With her right hand she swept the brown tignon from her grandmother's head, allowing the silver strands to scatter across the pillow. She flung the tignon onto the floor.

"You're no longer Marie Laveau. I am. Give me all the knowledge, all your anger, all the pain. Willingly I'll take it so that your own soul and mind can be free to die."

Using her fingers, she combed out her grandmother's

hair and loosened the layers of clothes that held the weak body together. Joints collapsed in upon themselves causing folds in the loose, weathered flesh.

"When you wake, it will be to ready yourself for the eternal sleep."

Chapter Seventy-three

Marie indelicately smacked her lips and felt for Igor's pulse. Ah, there she found it. He'd live to drink away another day of his life.

The bedclothes, tattered to begin with, were totally shredded, and under his hip an unrecognizable sticky puddle spread across the mattress. His hirsute body lay sprawled across most of the bed. The hair camouflaged several scars that had whitened his olive flesh. She wondered what had caused the awful gashes. Knife wounds? Perhaps a bad motor vehicle accident? They seemed to have been too deep to have been simple whip marks. She shrugged her shoulders and sat leaning her back against the peeling wall of the room.

Suz and Lola had become skittish when they saw Igor's abode. The front door with the boarded-up window they accepted as exciting. The funky hallway smell of jambalaya, rubbing alcohol, and urine made them hesitate for only a moment. The creaky steps and broken banister set a mood. But when he opened the door to his apartment and something scuttled under the radiator, they wouldn't cross the threshold.

Pets? No, he had no pets, he informed the young girls. She doubted that the girls had recognized the rat turd in the hallway, but the odor of wet fur couldn't be missed. They literally turned and ran when a long snout and two shiny eyes appeared poking out below the radiator.

She slapped Igor on the chest in sympathy and began to search for her clothes. She never found her fishnet stockings, not wanting to probe under any of the furniture.

Chapter Seventy-four

"Grandmother."

Marie Laveau pulled out of her trance and looked at the woman kneeling next to her. Her granddaughter's face looked pensive but tired. The wan flesh drooped heavy on her cheekbones. Dark circles under her eyes gave her an otherworldly look. Her turned-down lips made her look resigned.

"Marie Laveau," whispered the grandmother.

She took her granddaughter's hand, noticing the dirty, uneven nails.

"I'm happy you came back. I will soon meet the spirits and become one of them. I need you to continue."

"Remember, I am the last."

"What do doctors know? We have herbs and spells. . . ."

"I won't let you die in denial. I will never have a child."

"But you're wrong. You'll have Sade's babe fully grown and she will keep you company."

"You mean to pass Liliana's spirit onto me?"

"But you may never let Sade know. Let him believe she has been freed."

"Why make the girl suffer?"

"When you come to the end of your life, you must find Sade and let her spirit wreak havoc with him. Mold her into the perfect weapon. Remind her often of her father's sins. Make confusion reign."

"I'd rather stake Sade."

"No, no. Father and daughter must again be reunited. You should see how he denies Liliana, even threatens to destroy her if she attempts to come back in a tangible body."

"Can she?"

"Very unlikely. As feeble as I am, I can control her."

"Can we not put the poor woman's soul to rest? I can call her back when I'm ready to die."

"No, she will become too passive, perhaps even hard to reach. You must call her frequently, make sure she never forgets."

"And what of the other work I need to do? All my energy should be put into helping the sick and needy. This Liliana would only be a distraction."

The crone pulled herself up into a seated position, leaning her back against the headboard of the bed.

"Fill every hour of the day with your magic and your energy will grow stronger and stronger. Find the best way you can use Liliana's spirit. Include her in the daily work that you undertake. Allow her to take away the miseries of the sick. Let her carry the infections until she has become so bloated she reeks of pain. Let that be the final gift she gives to her father."

"And how will I finally pay for the evil I set in motion?"

"Evil? You are serving the vengeful gods that keep the

balance in this world," she said, raising her hand to touch the granddaughter's cheek, but the young woman turned away, tears glistening in her eyes. "Sade will come to you and ask what has happened to his precious child and you must be able to lie. Strip him of any doubts he may have. Let him think you've set him free of his greatest sin. Good and evil share the same space. They mingle together in each of us. No soul exists that hasn't been shaded by their dark deeds."

The granddaughter turned back to her grandmother.

"Then even Sade has good in him."

"But the good can only be freed if he pays the penalty for all the evil he has done."

"But what of Liliana? What is she paying for?"

"For being his daughter."

"She didn't choose her father. She may not even have chosen to be a vampire."

"But she chose to exist as a vampire and to acknowledge her paternity. She has never denied her father. She has sought to be with him. Longs for his love even though she knows the horrors he has committed."

"She is loyal as I am to you."

"When have you known me to hurt the innocent or blacken the souls of my brothers and sisters?"

Chapter Seventy-five

Sade awoke from a dreamless sleep, but felt no more rested than when he had been dreaming. His Liliana had been silenced at least for now. He knew she could be called back at the whim of a vengeful woman.

He paced the small apartment, wishing he could tear down the walls, take away the suffocating closeness of New Orleans. Even if he ripped apart the building, he'd never find release. Not from his daughter. Never from his daughter. She waited just out of his reach. He would only be able to squeeze the life from the conduit that promised the possibility of Liliana's return. Marie Laveau could reap vengeance from her grave through her twisted progeny.

He looked at a blank wall and saw the figure of Liliana take shape. Her eyes accusatory, her arms stretched out in supplication, and the two tiny dots upon her throat deepening into festering sores. He closed his eyes, but she still stood before him.

She promised to make him love her again, and with

that promise she doomed his days and nights to regret. Perhaps the only regret he would ever have.

His head hurt and his eyes grew bleary as he tried to free himself of his daughter's image.

"Louis."

He turned and saw his mother-in-law, Marie, closing the front door behind her.

"Have you tried to sleep yet?" she asked, her walk casual, her body movements relaxed. "Have you been dreaming?"

As she moved closer to him, the smell of blood grew stronger. Fresh blood.

"What's the matter, Louis?"

"You've just fed."

"Sorry, the man didn't offer takeout or I would have brought some for you."

The rich odor surrounded him. Liliana's blood had been the sweetest he had ever tasted, and as the blood flowed down his throat, her scent had inspired him to share his own with her. So long ago, yet here now in his memory.

Marie wrapped her hands around his neck and pressed her body to his.

"I could share some of my own blood with you, sweetheart, if . . ." Her eyes sparkled with lust.

His expression soured.

"Such a face, Louis. You'd think I had offered you that old crone's blood."

He tried to pull away, but she held him fast.

"I've never seen you this frazzled and unable to act before. Did you dream of Liliana again?"

He shook his head.

"But you did rest?"

"Yes. The death sleep came to me."

"Are you disappointed Liliana didn't show up in a dream?"

"As long as Marie Laveau is alive, I never will know whether my child will test my love for her again."

Marie dropped her arms to her sides. "Then you need to destroy Marie Laveau. Not just the old woman, but her granddaughter too."

He walked away from her and opened the window, allowing the street noise to block his thoughts. The smell of the river, booze, sweets, and mortals turned his stomach. A quarter moon dangled in the night sky looking precarious and soiled by the drifting clouds.

"Never before have I seen you hesitate," she said. "Why?"

Sade continued to stare out the window. His mother-in-law moved closer. Her shadow hung on the wall beside him.

"If the Vodou Queen and her granddaughter are made to disappear, then the connection to Liliana would surely be severed. If not, each death sleep you seek will be shrouded with anticipation and promise. A little girl could throw her arms around you. You could hear the tinkle of her laughter. Or maybe you would find her in her budding woman's body, tempting and luscious. A dream, you would think. Only a figment of the woman she could have been. What would you do? Make love to her? Or stay a chaste distance so that you could admire?

"Liliana was and could still be everything for you, Louis. Child, mate, succor when you needed a blind love. That's why you desire her so much."

Sade whipped back his right arm and drove it through the window's upper pane of glass. Shattering, the pieces of glass rained down on the tourists in the street. He looked down and saw fingers pointing at him. Strangers milled out of reach decrying his actions.

"Hey, buddy, sober up," yelled a middle-aged man with a baby in his arms.

Others ran across the street to the opposite sidewalk with their hands covering the tops of their heads.

He stared back, seeing motion but no specific features. When he recaptured control, he felt wetness on his knuckles and a soothing stream of flesh wiping the pain away. He looked down to see his mother-in-law holding his wrist and licking the blood from the cuts the glass had made.

Freeing his hand, he turned to the doorway and left.

Let the high praises of God be in their mouth, and a two-
edged sword in their hand;
To execute vengeance upon the heathen, and punishments
upon the people.

—Psalm 149:6–7

Chapter Seventy-six

Over and over the granddaughter practiced the coded symbols that enabled Liliana to follow this path back to the room in which she stood. If Liliana became lost anywhere along the way, Marie Laveau might not be able to find the girl again.

The crone pulled the drapes across the windows and announced that the time had come. She had nothing else to pass to her granddaughter except this one last spirit.

The crone passed a painted clay bowl half filled with cornmeal to the new Vodou Queen, whose hands shook as she accepted. As if on command, Hope slithered into the room from a dark corner. The snake appeared to melt free from a wall almost the same color as its skin.

The granddaughter had attired herself in her grandmother's old silk and lace. The tignon she wore, spotted with blood and animal juices, once had bound up the old woman's hair. Her feet were bare except for delicate drawings representing the gods. Set high up, the statue of the

Blessed Mother looked down upon the ritual, a scapula laced through her plaster hands.

"I once knew a priest who told me that I would go straight to Hell upon my death. He said Lucifer would be waiting by my deathbed counting the seconds before being able to snatch up my soul. But once set free, my soul wouldn't have far to go because the devil's fiery hands would escort my black soul to Hell." The crone smiled. "At the time he was an old man and I only middle-aged with many years to go. I sniffed at him and walked away, discounting all that he said for I had time to kneel in penance, plenty of time."

"An Act of Contrition and a rosary would gain you time in Purgatory, Grandmother."

"I can't ask forgiveness for what I must do. I would only be committing another sin."

"The greatest sin is despair."

"It is not despair I feel, Marie Laveau."

The granddaughter's spine stiffened at the name.

The crone bowed to the new Marie Laveau.

"No, I am repaying a long-standing debt. Only, it was easy to take on this way of life when my body reverberated with the confidence health brings. Now there is no more time left to borrow. I must pay the Lord what he is owed."

"Confess your sins, Grandmother, and the Lord will forgive."

"The Old Man knows what my sins are. It's repentance he wants me to feel. But I'm not sorry for anything that I've done. I followed your command, Marie Laveau, and I had no other choice." The crone began to make the sign of the cross, then stopped. "Do you think that old priest was right?"

"He was a sinner just like you and me, Grandmother. He made mistakes. He didn't truly know the will of God."

"Yes. You are wise, Marie Laveau. Thank you for sharing your strength with me." The crone bowed her head.

But the granddaughter didn't believe she was wise. Her weakness made her legs shake and caused her palms to sweat. Still, she moved into the ritual position while rubbing the coarse meal between her fingers.

When the silence of the room filled her with dread, she began drawing the vévé, dropping the cornmeal into a pattern, making a design that called Liliana to her. Her grandmother hummed and tapped out a ritual song so softly that Hope's motion as the snake drew closer to the vévé almost drowned out the musical sounds.

The candlelight flickered and several of the candles were snuffed out. Cold breezes blew the granddaughter's garments around her body, but never touched the fine lines of her drawing. Coiled into a ball, the snake waited just beyond the developing vévé.

When the last bit of cornmeal completed the design, the granddaughter's body quivered and the snake rushed forward to scatter the activated energy of the vévé.

The granddaughter experienced the worst sadness she had ever known. The cold chill flowing through her body chilled not only her heart, but also her thoughts.

"Liliana." She softly spoke the name.

She heard a howl that sounded far worse than any trapped animal had ever made. Hesitating to touch the spirit, the granddaughter dropped the bowl onto the floor. The echo of the shattering pottery stung her ears. The smell of blood assaulted her senses, and she looked up to see her grandmother's slashed wrists emptying blood onto the vévé, feeding the spirit.

Cautiously, the granddaughter's soul and mind reached into the pit of her own being to touch the spirit of Liliana.

"Liliana, I am Marie Laveau. Remember me?"

"You're different," Liliana replied.

"But the same," the granddaughter answered.

"Your hold on me is weak. You don't have the conviction you once had."

The granddaughter shivered and looked to her grandmother, but the old woman was no longer in control. The crone could only spill her blood in sacrifice.

"I will lead you back into this world and eventually back to your father."

"I've met my father, old . . ." Liliana stopped. "You were old, and now . . . Now you smell of inexperience. Inexperience and something else."

"I've come only to introduce myself to you, Liliana."

"You too are sad like me. You've lost someone."

The granddaughter stuttered out loud. The words rippled her lips, but her voice fell into heavy silence.

"Whom have you lost?" Liliana asked.

The granddaughter reminded herself that now Marie Laveau and she were one. The child she remembered being never existed. The games she played never for fun. She whispered "Marie Laveau" as a mantra, linking the two words as if they were one.

She staggered under the raging storm that built inside her.

"I . . . I am in control," she reminded the spirit. Fingers clutched her body and bile rose up from her stomach, splattering the room with the gelatinous mucus.

The smell of blood and vomit made her rock back and forth on the balls of her feet. She caught her breath in short pants until she almost felt that she need not breathe anymore.

"I never wanted to be you, Grandmother," she said, staring into the crone's eyes.

Old fingers wrapped around her forearms.

"But you've always been me." She watched the ancient purple lips pronounce the words. The crone's blood fell onto her flesh and a hunger so vast overtook her. Her tongue slipped between her lips, and she bowed her head to taste the blood. With renewed strength, the crone forced her chin upward away from the freshly stained skin.

"You possess the spirit, not the other way around," the crone reminded her. "You are Marie Laveau, the strongest Vodou Queen in this world. Spirits kneel at your feet awaiting your words, ready to fulfill your desires."

The pressure on her chest lessened. Her lungs once again accepted air, but too soon she felt winter frost her innards once again.

"Curse you, foul blood-sucker," the crone screamed. She raised her fists into her granddaughter's face. "You cannot steal away the spirit of Marie Laveau. Give back her body." The crone staggered backward and reached for the terrarium, lifting it high into the air and smashing it against the wood floor with superhuman power. With carelessness caused by her speed, she grabbed the rattler too near the head, giving the snake the opportunity to sink its venom into her flesh.

The granddaughter saw the bead of blood flow from the crone's wound.

"Grandmother." The blood hunger took control and

she recognized it reflected in her grandmother's eyes. The crone offered her the poisonous snake.

"Don't let her back," the crone said. "Destroy your body before Liliana can return."

The snake writhed within the crone's hold and the granddaughter could see the disappointment in her grandmother's eyes. But the granddaughter had already lost control of her limbs. Her hands did not respond to the gift. Instead the crone fell to the floor gripping the tormented rattler.

Oh that I were
Where I would be,
Then would I be
Where I am not;
But where I am
There must I be,
And where I would be
I cannot.

—English Nursery Rhyme

Chapter Seventy-seven

Sade followed the stench of blood and vomit up to the second floor finding the dimly lit living room hushed in silence. The ancient Marie Laveau lay on the floor, her mouth agape, her fingers rigid with the small rattler pushing free of her hands. The tremors wracking her body proved her to be in the final throes of death.

He moved farther into the room to see her eyes, which shined like crystal glass fresh from the fire. Her face seemed made of leather.

He heard a gasp, and turned to see the granddaughter staring down at the rattler that moved toward her toes. Without thinking, Sade smashed his heel down on the rattler's head.

"I didn't come here to save your life," he said to her. She gave no response, her body statuesquely beautiful in the candlelight. "I came to take both your lives."

The granddaughter looked at him and tried to speak,

but not finding her voice, she tried to express language with her hands, but they fluttered too much in the air.

"It is finished for your grandmother. Marie Laveau cannot haunt me anymore except in the guise of your flesh."

She looked at her hands and fumbled with the silk and lace of her garments, trying, it seemed, desperately to recognize the old rags.

"I pity you in your loss, mademoiselle. I know the tragedy of losing someone who is loved."

He watched the granddaughter shake violently, and heard her let out a piercing cry of grief. She fell to her knees, ripping the ancient seams as she hit the floor.

"And will you allow her to live, Louis?"

He turned to find his mother-in-law stepping delicately around a large coiled snake.

"Pathetic," he pronounced, looking back at the granddaughter.

"But is she risk-free? Can she recapture her grandmother's magic? And if she does, will she seek you out again?"

"You want me to kill her."

"That's why you came here. Why wait? Don't torture the poor young woman with your procrastination, Louis. Do it quickly and let her rejoin the decrepit old witch lying there on the floor."

The large snake hissed, raising its head to touch the air with its tongue.

"I doubt that's a friendly gesture."

"Its mistress is dead. Give it a chance to mourn."

The granddaughter fell to her side and rolled onto her back, staring straight up at the ceiling. Slight quivering movements roiled across her body.

"Kill her, Louis, or I will."

"Her blood is too spoiled for me. Take her and spare me from drinking down her filth." He walked to the door, noticing that the snake had disappeared.

He heard his mother-in-law cackle with glee as she squatted down near her prey.

"She's really not so putrid, Louis, but then I've never been the target of her rage. Actually her skin is soft and smooth, but how very cold she is. I would almost think that she's already dead."

He looked back at the two women. One moving her lips, searching for words, the other licking her lips with her tongue.

The mother-in-law ripped the young woman's clothes, revealing a shapely taut body. A body not stung into collapse by the years.

"She's very beautiful. A terrible waste." She looked up at Sade. "Are you sure you wouldn't like one more go?"

He walked back to the women.

"There are marvelous things we could do with her before sapping her dry, Louis."

"You're suggesting a ménage à trois. A sly way to ravish my body."

She smirked. "A delightful way to pass our last night in New Orleans."

Bits and pieces of words escaped the granddaughter's mouth.

"Oh, hush, child. Stop complaining. We'll do our very best to appreciate . . ." Her hand rounded the granddaughter's breast, tweaking the nipple. "Every inch of your flesh."

Mesmerized, Sade sat down on the floor ready to watch the two women at play.

His mother-in-law pulled away what few rags still hugged the granddaughter's body and whisked the tignon from her head.

Sade caught the mother-in-law grinning at him while she removed her own clothes. Her bare skin, porcelain white, complemented the granddaughter's tawny flesh. With one hand she touched herself, and with the other she played with the granddaughter's pubic hair while leaning forward to kiss his lips.

He tasted the stale blood from her prior victim, the copper taste raw against his tongue. His fingers opened the buttons on his shirt, and she raised her hands to assist in removing his clothes.

He heard a tiny voice say, "No." But so frail was the sound that he could easily ignore the plea.

"Yes," said the mother-in-law, taking his engorged meat in her hands and grinning down at their helpless victim.

Weakly, the granddaughter raised a hand toward him, and he lifted it to his lips, kissing the palm and nibbling the long fingers. He remembered the feel and taste of her body from Paris and the sweet juices that aided in his thrusts to dig deeper into her.

"Once more, mademoiselle, before you find eternal rest with your dear grandmother." He leaned down to taste her lips as those same lips shaped the word "Father." He heard the word spoken and his stomach retched. He faltered briefly before wrapping his hands around her throat.

"You can't." His mother-in-law grasped his hands.

"Father."

"She's done it. She's come back to us," the mother-in-law shouted in his ear.

"No, she mocks us. This is not Liliana."

The prone woman raised her hands to his ring.

"Will you give me your ring once again? Will you give it to me a third time?"

"I said I would destroy you if you came to me in the flesh, Liliana."

"No, Louis. Please." His mother-in-law kept stabbing at his fingers with her long nails until he finally released his hold.

He looked around the room for a slender piece of wood or even a pipe made of metal. Something to drive into her heart. But he couldn't see clearly. The room seemed cluttered with worthless debris. He spied the Virgin Mother watching over the scene. A crucifix. She had to have a crucifix somewhere. He rose to his feet and searched the walls from room to room until he found a crucifix on the bedroom wall. It almost slipped from his hands as he took it down.

Raging, he reentered the living room and saw the two women clinging to each other. The darker woman held strips of rags to her body attempting to hide her nakedness.

"Louis, this is really Liliana. She has told me things that only Liliana would know. Childhood nicknames for her dolls. The silly, secret wish we made together one Christmas. This is our Liliana."

The splintered wood of the crucifix jabbed his flesh. Sade broke the crossbeam from the crucifix, leaving a long firm piece of wood.

"Louis, you can't. . . ."

He walked toward the women as his mother-in-law positioned herself in front of Liliana.

"I won't let you destroy her."

Calmly he reached down and grabbed a firm hold of his mother-in-law's black hair, pulling her away from his daughter.

"I see only a woman who would destroy me," he said. "A woman I bedded long ago who refused to die."

Liliana rose to her knees.

"Father, would you rid yourself of me so quickly without even a final paternal kiss?"

The lilt of the voice was not Marie Laveau's. The eyes were softer than the Vodou Queen's had been. She tried to smile, but her lips trembled too much.

He used his right hand to push her back onto the floor and raised the stake in his left hand. One final good-bye and his life would be restored to him. The stake weighed heavily in his hand, but he centered his sight on her left breast under which her heart beat.

With a mighty force he plunged downward, his aim finding the crippled dead body of Marie Laveau.

"You brought this upon me," he shouted, taking the stake out only to more forcefully pound it back into the crone's heart.

He sensed a flourish of movement to his left and fell forward, barely missing the crone's desiccated body.

When the women came to him, they were dressed and brought his clothes with them.

"Come, Louis, we can go home now. Let's go back to Paris. We've been given a gift and should be celebrating."

He would go back to his coffin and take a long, dreamless sleep, he promised himself.

"Father, let me help you."

The words stabbed his heart, but he allowed her to slip his shirt over his shoulders.

"Liliana, my treasure," he said, looking up into the gentleness of her eyes.

TAINTED BLOOD

MARY ANN MITCHELL

The infamous Marquis de Sade has lived through the centuries. This master vampire cares little for his human playthings, seeking them out only for his amusement and nourishment. Once his dark passion and his bloodlust are sated, he moves on, leaving another drained and discarded toy in his wake.

Now Sade is determined to find the woman who made his life hell—and destroy her. His journey leads him to a seemingly normal suburban American house. But the people who live there are undead. And when the notorious Marquis meets the all-American family of vampires, the resulting culture clash will prove fatal. But for whom?

- -

Dorchester Publishing Co., Inc.
P.O. Box 6640 **$6.99 US/$8.99 CAN**
Wayne, PA 19087-8640 **__ 5091-9**

Please add $2.50 for shipping and handling for the first book and $.75 for each book thereafter. NY and PA residents, please add appropriate sales tax. No cash, stamps, or C.O.D.s. Prices and availability subject to change.
Canadian orders require $2.00 extra postage and must be paid in U.S. dollars through a U.S. banking facility.

Name______________________________________
Address____________________________________
City____________________ State______ Zip__________
E-mail_____________________________________
I have enclosed $__________ in payment for the checked book(s).
Payment <u>must</u> accompany all orders. __ Check here for a free catalog.

CHECK OUT OUR WEBSITE! www.dorchesterpub.com

WOUNDS

JEMIAH JEFFERSON

Jemiah Jefferson exploded onto the horror scene with her debut novel, *Voice of the Blood*, the most original, daring, and erotically frightening vampire novel in years. Now her seductive, provocative world of darkness is back.

Vampire Daniel Blum imagines himself the most ruthless, savage creature in New York City, if not the world. He once feasted on the blood of Nazi Germany and left a string of shattered lovers behind him. But now the usual thrill of seduction and murder has begun to wear off. Until he meets Sybil, the strange former stripper whose mind is the first he's ever found that he cannot read or manipulate. . . .

___4998-8 $6.99 US/$8.99 CAN

Dorchester Publishing Co., Inc.
P.O. Box 6640
Wayne, PA 19087-8640

Please add $2.50 for shipping and handling for the first book and $0.75 for each additional book. NY and PA residents, add appropriate sales tax. No cash, stamps, or C.O.D.s. All Canadian orders require $2.00 for shipping and handling and must be paid in U.S. dollars. Prices and availability subject to change. **Payment must accompany all orders.**

Name ____

Address ______________________________________

City ____________________ State _____ Zip __________

E-mail

I have enclosed $ ________ in payment for the checked book(s).

❑Please send me a free catalog.

CHECK OUT OUR WEBSITE at www.dorchesterpub.com!

VOICE OF THE BLOOD

JEMIAH JEFFERSON

Ariane is desperate for some change, some excitement to shake things up. She has no idea she is only one step away from a whole new world–a world of darkness and decay, of eternal life and eternal death. But once she falls prey to Ricari she will learn more about this world than she ever dreamt possible. More than anyone should dare to know . . . if they value their soul. For Ricari's is the world of the undead, the vampire, a world far beyond the myths and legends that the living think they know. From the clubs of San Francisco to a deserted Hollywood hotel known as Rotting Hxall, the denizens of this land of darkness hold sway over the night. Bur a seductive and erotic as these predators may be, Ariane will soon discover that a little knowledge can be a very dangerous thing indeed.

___4830-2 $6.99 US/$8.99 CAN

Dorchester Publishing Co., Inc.
P.O. Box 6640
Wayne, PA 19087-8640

Please add $2.50 for shipping and handling for the first book and $.75 for each book thereafter. NY, NYC, and PA residents, please add appropriate sales tax. No cash, stamps, or C.O.D.s. All orders shipped within 6 weeks via postal service book rate. Canadian orders require $2.00 extra postage and must be paid in U.S. dollars through a U.S. banking facility.

Name___________________________
Address_________________________
City________________ State______ Zip________
I have enclosed $________ in payment for the checked book(s).
Payment <u>must</u> accompany all orders. ☐ Please send a free catalog.
CHECK OUT OUR WEBSITE! www.dorchesterpub.com

THE TRAVELING VAMPIRE SHOW

RICHARD LAYMON

It's a hot August morning in 1963. All over the rural town of Grandville, tacked to the power poles and trees, taped to store windows, flyers have appeared announcing the one-night-only performance of The Traveling Vampire Show. The promised highlight of the show is the gorgeous Valeria, the only living vampire in captivity.

For three local teenagers, two boys and a girl, this is a show they can't miss. Even though the flyers say no one under eighteen will be admitted, they're determined to find a way. What follows is a story of friendship and courage, temptation and terror, when three friends go where they shouldn't go, and find much more than they ever expected.

__4850-7 $6.99 US/$8.99 CAN

Dorchester Publishing Co., Inc.
P.O. Box 6640
Wayne, PA 19087-8640

Please add $2.50 for shipping and handling for the first book and $.75 for each book thereafter. NY, NYC, and PA residents, please add appropriate sales tax. No cash, stamps, or C.O.D.s. All orders shipped within 6 weeks via postal service book rate. Canadian orders require $2.00 extra postage and must be paid in U.S. dollars through a U.S. banking facility.

Name______________________________
Address______________________________
City________________ State______ Zip________
I have enclosed $__________ in payment for the checked book(s).
Payment must accompany all orders. ☐ Please send a free catalog.
CHECK OUT OUR WEBSITE! www.dorchesterpub.com

RICHARD LAYMON

ENDLESS NIGHT

Jody is pretty tough for a sixteen-year-old girl. That's the only reason she's still alive—for now. She was sleeping over at her friend Evelyn's house when a group of killers broke in and tried to slaughter everyone. She saw Evelyn spitted on a spear, but Jody managed to escape, along with Evelyn's little brother, Andy.

Simon was one of the killers that gruesome night. His friends have left it up to him to find the only living witnesses to their massacre. Or else they'll butcher his family next. But Simon has his own reasons for wanting to get his hands on Jody. . . .

Dorchester Publishing Co., Inc.
P.O. Box 6640 ____5184-2
Wayne, PA 19087-8640 $7.99 US/$9.99 CAN

Please add $2.50 for shipping and handling for the first book and $.75 for each additional book. NY and PA residents, add appropriate sales tax. No cash, stamps, or CODs. Canadian orders require an extra $2.00 for shipping and handling and must be paid in U.S. dollars. Prices and availability subject to change. **Payment must accompany all orders.**

Name: ____________________

Address: ____________________

City: ____________ State: ________ Zip: ________

E-mail: ____________________

I have enclosed $__________ in payment for the checked book(s).

CHECK OUT OUR WEBSITE! www.dorchesterpub.com.

____ *Please send me a free catalog.*

RICHARD LAYMON

BODY RIDES

Neal has been carrying a gun in his car lately—just to be safe. And it looks like it's a good thing he has. When he spots a woman tied naked to a tree and a man ready to kill her, he has no choice but to shoot the attacker. As a reward, the woman gives Neal something unimaginable.

Neal's reward is a bracelet. A very special bracelet. It enables its wearer to step inside other people, to see through their eyes, to feel whatever they feel. To take "body rides." But Neal has a big problem. The man he shot isn't dead. And he wants revenge. First he's going to finish what he started with the woman. Then he's going after Neal. . . .

Dorchester Publishing Co., Inc.
P.O. Box 6640
Wayne, PA 19087-8640

___5182-6
$7.99 US/$9.99 CAN

Please add $2.50 for shipping and handling for the first book and $.75 for each additional book. NY and PA residents, add appropriate sales tax. No cash, stamps, or CODs. Canadian orders require an extra $2.00 for shipping and handling and must be paid in U.S. dollars. Prices and availability subject to change. **Payment must accompany all orders.**

Name: ________________________________

Address: ________________________________

City: ________________ State: __________ Zip: __________

E-mail: ________________________________

I have enclosed $__________ in payment for the checked book(s).

For more information on these books, check out our website at www.dorchesterpub.com.

____ *Please send me a free catalog.*

ATTENTION BOOK LOVERS!

Can't get enough
of your favorite **HORROR**?

Call **1-800-481-9191** to:

— order books —

— receive a **FREE** catalog —

— join our book clubs to **SAVE 20%**! —

Open Mon.-Fri. 10 AM-9 PM EST

Visit
www.dorchesterpub.com
for special offers and inside
information on the authors you love.

We accept Visa, MasterCard or Discover®.